ALL GOD'S step CHILDREN

ALL GOD'S step CHILDREN

Yve S. Mari

Copyright © 2016 by Yve S. Mari.

Library of Congress Control Number: 2016919533
ISBN: Hardcover 978-1-5245-6360-8
Softcover 978-1-5245-6359-2
eBook 978-1-5245-6358-5

All rights reserved. No part of this book may be reproduced or transmitted in any form or by any means, electronic or mechanical, including photocopying, recording, or by any information storage and retrieval system, without permission in writing from the copyright owner.

This is a work of fiction. Names, characters, places and incidents either are the product of the author's imagination or are used fictitiously, and any resemblance to any actual persons, living or dead, events, or locales is entirely coincidental.

Edited by: Anne Daly Hagan, Melissa Li-Ng,
Heather C. Futral, Lauren L. Crawford
Cover design by Joy Osborn
Dove Media Marketing
Written by Y.Scott

Print information available on the last page.

Rev. date: 12/30/2016

To order additional copies of this book, contact:
Xlibris
1-888-795-4274
www.Xlibris.com
Orders@Xlibris.com
752977

DEDICATION

For those who refused to allow me to quit,
I owe you more than mere respect and gratitude:

William III and Dianne	Edwin and Bertha
Derek and Melissa	Leroy and Edna
Brian and Sharonda	Maurice and Jacque
Tennie and Jan	Paul and Faychon
Charles and Kris	Tom and Nancy
Peter and Debbie	Wm. Arline and Linda
Charles and Kris	Shannon and Janella
Christine and Ronnie	Scott and Molly
Stevens Family and Wilson Family	Ted and Mary

Vivian, Carrie, Floyd, Talya, Dana, Danielle, Denise,
Corinne, Yaa, Ryan, Robert, Daniel, Tangla, Mary,
Bertina, Marie, Ann Marie, Liz, Anissa,
Sherry, Jacob, Izamara, Adenike, Imre,
Guadalupe, Maria, Evette, Eric, Sue,
Andrea, Brian, Scott, Theresa,
Tony, Maude, JD,
and Genice.

FOREWORD

Throughout the ages, men have repeatedly enslaved the unsuspecting, the defenseless and the innocent without much opposition. That is what has made the institution of slavery a unique source of power on which men could constantly rely. It could be easily implemented into a hidden community. It could be brutally adopted from an abandoned creed. Slavery was to be embraced as long as the institution met one requirement. It must always benefit the oppressor. And the slave had to understand that they had no right to feelings, decisions or dreams because hope was an unaffordable luxury.

INTRODUCTION

"Males never failed to disappoint. They always found ways to live up to their proverbial characteristics. Males are cruel, dishonest and reckless. Males are thoughtless, angry and deficient. Males are unpredictable, predatory and selfish. Males are dangerous, exhaustive and violent. Yet, despite these truths, we could not ignore one simple fact. The male species were our "necessary" enemy if we were to survive and advance."

Eden was captivated by every word that Professor Raine stated. Much like her grandmother, Professor Raine passionately impressed these reminders upon her students. Eden stood quietly behind the crowd of students and officials gathered before her. She began to smile as she recalled a similar sentiment that her grandmother stressed during her childhood.

"As students, artists, scientists, professors, mothers, innovators, engineers, physicians, sisters, officials, attorneys, researchers, mentors and daughters, we have to do more than embrace an unconventional idea. If we are to survive, we must create a new world for ourselves by any means necessary. We have no choice. The men are bent on destruction, and the women and children are paying the ultimate price," her grandmother's words flooded her mind.

The roar of the applause throughout the lecture hall disrupts Eden's thoughts. Without hesitation, Eden joins the crowd in praising her grandmother. The admiration for her grandmother is evidenced in the great ovation from the students and the royals. It overwhelms Eden.

As the professor continues to speak, Eden immediately returns to her thoughts. "We have very little time to make very big changes in this very hostile world. If we are to establish a progressive, positive, purposeful, productive and possibly peaceful society, then we must force the males to become subservient to us. Enslaving them is the most viable option." She recalls the exact moment in her childhood when her grandmother made this declaration.

Deep in concentration, Eden pondered, "If grandmother had not rescued us from the male species, we would have all been destroyed. Slavery had to be the most viable option for everyone," Eden tried to reason as she peered at her grandmother. She then rubbed her forehead as if to alleviate the wrestling of the thoughts that were troubling her mind. "Slavery was our only option," she whispers to herself.

Males Created Nightmares...

Maybe it was memories of past nightmares or nightmares of the past. Either way, Eden never forgot her mother's attempts to try and hide the fear in her voice. Her mother instructed the girls to close their eyes. "Hold my hands," she said to them as they squeezed their eyelids together tightly. But no amount of darkness could erase the imbedded images of blood. Even when the girls covered their ears, they could not mute the screams.

The fear was beyond evident in their eyes. Other than covering their bodies with her own, Eden's mother could offer no real comfort from the explosions and gun firing surrounding them.

As the thickness of the smoke and haze engulfed their shelter, she knew the girls did not understand the fighting occurring outside. She especially knew that it did not matter how much they were all suffering. It was war and they were not allowed to ignore it. This was a war that had been designed to demand everyone's attention. The only thing that was made extremely clear to the girls was that being born female proved to be a tremendous crime.

Males Are To Bow...

The voice of the correspondent resonated from the vision panel inside the transport. "As expected, no criminal activity occurred today. All systems throughout the citadel are reported to be stable and sound," the correspondent broadcasts as her voice fades into the background. The transport arrives at the academy.

The dean of the academy approaches the council. Wearing the official academic garb, she greets each royal with a customary bow before guiding everyone inside.

All God's *step*-Children

The fresh scent of the corridor alone screamed success. Eden found it difficult to focus on what the dean was saying. "The loss of life was so intense that it seemed as though no one could claim true victory. Nevertheless, even though thirty years have passed since the war ended, we still pride ourselves on the strength and freedom that these women have afforded us," the dean stated. Eden was drawn to the historical images poured onto the walls.

The tour of the new facility continued. It was evident how much Eden admired the embodiment of each heroine in the paintings. She looked upon each of their abstract images with tears. Every portrait was labeled with each woman's name, age and specific act of bravery. Their sacrifice created this new world that Eden's grandmother envisioned and forcefully sought.

In her spirited tone, Professor Raine attempted to continue teaching. However, it was clear that the prestigious presence of the royals standing in the doorway was disturbing the girls. As she raised her eyeglasses atop her hair, Professor Raine in her thin pale frame was forced to suspend her lesson. The students smiled with unyielding delight at the visitors. She invited them into the lecture hall. Graciously, the council accepted while Professor Raine formally introduced each member. "Class, we are privileged to have very special guests from the royal court visiting. Please young ladies show them proper honor," Professor Raine urged.

The students arose from their seats and paid homage to the royals by bowing. Eden's grandmother received the most praise as any queen should. Dressed in royal garments, she was more than prepared to give a speech, but Eden shied away from the attention in humility.

The mere sight of the ambitious students dressed so uniformly in their navy and gold filled the council and

Eden's grandmother with tremendous pride. Polished, well-spoken and intelligent described these young and gifted females who were to be fully educated in order to lead and advance the new society.

Professor Raine was allowed to continue her lecture without further interruption. One student asked, "Why do the men always choose to solve problems with violence and force? Why don't they agree to talk and engage in a fair exchange of ideas?" The officials observed the dynamics of the class with great scrutiny.

At this, Professor Raine took a deep breath and reminded the girls that violence was part of the male genetic make-up. She stated, "Biological, chemical, psychological and sociological research has proven that the male species is more prone to ill-equipped reasoning. They operate more on impulsivity. It is rather complex to explain in a few sentences due to the illogical methods in which males use to process and operate." Professor Raine tried not to further confuse her impressionable young students.

Then one student countered, "Basically, what we can conclude is that the men cannot help themselves because it is their nature. Correct?" The other girls begin to murmur, laugh and nod in agreement. While the royal council continued to observe the dynamics of the class, Professor Raine regained their attention by explaining that this was the exact reason why the males could never again be trusted, let alone be allowed to make sound decisions regarding anyone's life including their own. "It is vital that we structure their lives for them for the sake of advancing our civilization," Professor Raine remarked.

The young girls began to clap. Eden glanced at her grandmother who was nodding in agreement to what Professor Raine was stating.

One student asserted, "None of us would ever want to reside in their world of chaos." More discussion followed as Grandmother silently gave Professor Raine a supportive nod of approval for the manner in which she answered the inquisitive female students.

As the activity among the class continued, Eden began to flashback to what she had experienced under the rule of men. That is when her heart began to race at the thought of the suffering. The words that her grandmother proclaimed echoed through her mind, "Slavery must be our only option." As she calms herself, Eden is brought back to the lecture when Professor Raine began to speak about familiar teachings.

"Whether the men fought to dominate control over land, oil, politics, water, diamonds, precious metals, territories, religion, women, drugs, skin color, weapons, food or power, their crimes against the environment, animals and humanity had reached beyond time and space. We had to stop the impact of their devastation before it was too late. There was only one way to stop the males. We had no choice but to enslave them all," Professor Raine declared. As these words were spoken, cheering and clapping erupted from every student and royal present in the hall. The ringing of the school bell brought the lecture to an end. The girls paid respect to each council member before they exited the classroom.

The officials took a moment to speak with Professor Raine. Meanwhile, Eden observed each student walking out of the hall and into the corridor. As the girls passed by, each male slave showed proper respect by bowing prostrate at their feet until each student departed.

Each male slave strategically positioned themselves far from any female student or staff other than the female guards as they had been instructed. The male slaves were not allowed to engage in eye contact.

Their enslavement had become beneficial to the new order. It had become the custom to command all males as slaves. However, Eden had great difficulty exercising such restrictions on the males. Yet, Eden trusted that her grandmother was right. The male slaves required great structure and discipline as any slave would.

No female would dare abuse or mistreat any male slave. It was against the decree. It was just a relief to know that the slaves feared the authority of the female guards.

Besides, Eden's grandmother said it would be more beneficial to show care and concern to the males. She felt strongly about treating the males with decency. Her hope was that they could be taught how to control their impulsivities and alleviate their inclinations to be violent. Grandmother believed that they could be slaves who could be taught to obey devoid methods of abuse. The past already proved that males could never be allowed to have any autonomy or authority over themselves or anyone else ever again.

As the tour of the campus ended, Eden tried to listen attentively to the engineers and the provost. All made thoughtful recommendations to the council regarding the newly designed campus.

However, Eden was more fascinated with observing her cousin, Ilya, who not only resembled their grandmother, but constantly strived to imitate their grandmother's leadership in every way. Ilya so desired to be like her and please her. Their grandmother knew how to lead the new civilization with grace.

Males Triggered Memories...

Eden watched from a distance as her cousin Ilya and grandmother bid their formal goodbyes to the students and staff. Ilya and grandmother seemed genetically designed for the purpose of drawing crowds. Ilya especially commanded attention with her striking red hair dancing in the breeze. As they departed the campus with their entourage, Eden elected a more discrete method of transport. She greeted the air transporter and requested to return to the palace.

The telecom was broadcasting the news while Eden mindlessly stared at the correspondent on the screen. After little time, her voice became meaningless background noise. Eden became more drawn to all the life taking place outside the transport window. The transport carried Eden by beautiful gardens and the lush greenery of parks. The female citizens found outside were adorned in flowy soft dresses of various colors. The only persons dressed in black were the guards. Eden took note of all the beauty of the women and the environment. Eden felt a peacefulness which allowed her to close her eyes and rest her forehead against the window. Memories of Eden's mother and Nanny began to comfort her.

As her mind begins to clear, Eden recalled the formal staunchness of her nanny, Ms. Vivian, barking orders to both her and her cousin early one morning. With her hair perfectly swept into a bun, she demanded of Ilya, "You must wear the required sash for school. Now hurry and get dressed!" The more Ms. Vivian yelled at them, the more dysfunctional and playful Eden and Ilya were. They were bonded seemingly in every way. "For ladies who are supposed to become our future rulers, you girls are extremely aloof!" Ms. Vivian exclaimed. Ilya whispered, "What does ah-luf mean?" Eden just laughed. At Ms. Vivian's prompting, Ilya and Eden rushed along the corridor.

It was no surprise to see Princess Dianne standing at the end of the corridor to greet them. Reserved in dress and manner, Princess Dianne knew how to command the attention of the girls with her tall thin frame.

Both Eden and Ilya offered a half-hearted apology as they tried to avoid her stare of shame. "Don't you both own wristwatches, extremely expensive watches at that?" Princess Dianne asked. Basically, their routine lateness was driving Eden's mother insane. Princess Dianne would simply shake her head in disappointment as she emphasized their names, "Eden and Ilya!" Eden however was welcomed the memory of her mother shaking her head back and forth. Watching her mother's course thick hair move as one grand ball of fluff amused the girls.

Nevertheless, regardless of her upset with the girls, Princess Dianne clearly and equally loved them. She questioned, "How are you girls ever going to be rulers who maintain a standard of integrity and responsibility when you hardly arrive at school on time?"

The girls in their seven and nine year old bodies would lower their heads in shame as they were reminded that it is never okay for any princess to be tardy. In unison they would resound, "Yes ma'am". In her role as Princess Dianne, she always granted them forgiveness. But, as mom, she showered the girls with hugs.

Even though Princess Dianne was not Ilya's birth mother, Ilya was as much her daughter as was Eden. It was not a huge undertaking for Princess Dianne to adopt Ilya as her own because Ilya was her niece. Ilya was the only child of her older sister, Princess Dana. Neither Eden's grandmother nor Eden's mother, Princess Dianne, did ever speak of much of Dana because Princess Dana died tragically and immediately after giving birth to Ilya.

And although Ilya was older, Eden's mother and grandmother were extremely protective of her. Even prior to the war, their grandmother heavily monitored Ilya's interactions especially with males. As a child, Ilya preferred to engage in athletic sports like many of the young males around her did.

The queen was very uneasy about allowing Ilya to spend time with any male. However, Princess Dianne did allow Ilya to maintain her friendship with a young boy of a servant named Nealon. He seemed to be one of the only people who could help Ilya as a young girl channel the fire that seemed to rage inside of her. Ilya seemed to listen to him. He not only taught Ilya how to swim, how to ride a horse, and how to shoot an arrow. He also taught her how to laugh.

Yet, it was Princess Dianne who made certain that both girls received tremendous training in every subject ranging from science, engineering, mathematics and mechanics to psychology, art, music, languages, economics and history. Princess Dianne knew how to inspire unity, courage and hope in every female in order to ensure they would all receive proper education.

It was often said that Eden had inherited her mother's patience, integrity, grace, discernment, self-discipline and fairness. However, her cousin Ilya was the more brave and daring one. She had an authoritative and passionate presence which never left her at a loss for words. Princess Dianne recognized the strong personality that Ilya possessed. She did her best to foster her talents in order to fully equip her to lead one day.

Ilya sought to impress Eden's mother in every way, even more so than her grandmother. That was the very heart of Ilya. However, when Eden's mother died during the war, the merciful part of Ilya's heart also died. Her death proved an even greater trauma to Ilya more than the effects of the war. It may have been the trigger that caused Ilya to harden her heart.

Their Decision...

The new dawn began to expose their hiding place outside the tall wrought iron city gates of the citadel. With her long dark hair absorbing her tears, Elizabeth hugs Lliam tightly as she trembles with fear. "It is too dangerous for us to try and survive out here. We have no more family. We only have each other. And I refuse to lose you or our son," Elizabeth says as she cradles their baby. "Maybe there is hope for his survival inside those majestic walls. Maybe they can better protect him and care for him at least for a while," she tries to persuade.

In great calm, Lliam reassures with a hug in order to alleviate her worry. He has no doubt that GOD blessed them with this baby for a purposeful reason. Lliam gently pushes her hair behind her ears and wipes her tears. With his calloused dry hands he holds his son's tiny fingers. They are fragile. Lliam states, "Our son will help deliver us all. We must believe that," Lliam urges. Elizabeth nods in agreement.

Males Inside Their World...

The palace hall was filled with the smell of breakfast and the sounds of intricate conversation. It was supposed to be a moderate forecast that late March. Yet, the sun was providing much warmth this spring season of 2084.

All God's *step*-Children

In grandeur, the queen entered the dining hall. All the officials arose to bow. Male slaves were to remain prostrate until they were instructed to rise and continue their duties. The female guards scrutinized their every move.

Once all the officials were seated, their attention was focused toward the mainframe screen. Each female broadcaster presented their various reports regarding the citadel. Their commentaries included economics, education, environment, finance, trade, meteorology, industry, healthcare, military, legal and infrastructure. Each individual report proved favorable.

The officials were pleased with the news, which only added to the already pleasant atmosphere in the dining hall. As each female official shared in the joy of morning conversation, the chief security officer provided her report on the statistics regarding her department. Once again her report was brief because the criminal activity was non-existent.

Even the chief medical examiner could not expand on her clinical report because any form of infection or disease was equally non-existent.

The primary reason for the lack of crime, disease and violence was the fact that all the males were enslaved. Freedom of any male was tremendous violation of the law mandated by the queen. Males had to be constantly controlled. It was the only way to prevent them from wreaking chaos and causing harm.

Ilya insisted that her grandmother appoint Vayl to the position of Chief of Security against her grandmother's better judgment. Vayl was one of Ilya's most reliable and trusted best friends. Yet, no one was more loyal to Ilya than her only other best friend, Amblin. Ilya heavily relied upon both Vayl and Amblin as if they were her very own blood sisters. Amblin and Vayl both had long silky blonde locks which would often confuse anyone who approached them from behind as to which was which. With Ilya in her lean athleticism dominating their tight feminine force, their bond seemed unbreakable.

Vayl reported that all male containment units were stable. "However, I do have concerns regarding the perimeter. Apparently, there is rumor that rebel males have been spotted in nearby forests. They could be a potential threat," Vayl stated.

The queen inquired if any breaks in the perimeter or if any assaults had occurred? Vayl stated that no attacks on citizens were reported. "These unidentified males have yet to be contained. Their images had been captured on our security system but no identification has been confirmed," Vayl stated.

The queen recommended that no one be allowed to venture outside the city gates until further notice. "Alert all royals and citizens, but do it without causing panic or alarm. It is vital that everyone feel protected and safe," the queen insists. Vayl nodded in understanding before directing her troops. While the briefing continued, another official inquired about the whereabouts of Eden.

Males Cannot Be Family...

Eden could barely speak. It was as if she were choking. She continued to fight in order to move through the crowd. Yet, it seemed as though the ground was giving way beneath her feet. All she could do is watch helplessly as the male slave stood elevated on the platform before the crowd. There was a noose tied around his neck. He was awaiting execution and she could no longer forcibly move her body towards him to help. Eden falls to the ground in frustration.

The shouts from the crowd became more and more muffled. A hand suddenly rested heavily on her shoulder. Eden turned around only to be confronted by an enchanting blonde woman. She was dressed blindingly in white. The woman warned, "Do not allow the blood of the innocent to be shed." Eden awakens gasping for air. She places her hands on her neck only to realize that she was dreaming.

Eden stood up and moved quickly towards the sunlight on her balcony to further catch her breath. She allowed the morning rays to shine directly into her dark eyes. She allowed the soft cool breeze to gently move her thick ringlets from her face. The fresh morning air begins to revive her. Quietly she begins to calm down from memory of the dream. The dream felt so real. Yet, the more she stared out beyond the city walls, the more she found relief. She once again allowed her mind to wonder as she looked out over the citadel and thought about what existed beyond her certain world.

"Excuse me princess!" a gentle deep male voice respectfully inquires. Eden came back to her senses when she heard that familiar voice. She smiled before she even turned around. "Good morning Mr. Shale", Eden said as she gripped his wrinkled old hands. "Don't you even dare think about bowing down to me, Mr. Shale," Eden commanded. Mr. Shale was more than 70 years old and could barely move with drive. With his touch of arthritis, there was no way Eden would allow him to bow. Besides, he was family to her and he survived more than his fair share of tragedy even before the war.

"Princess you know you are not supposed to have any physical contact with the slaves. What would your grandmother say if she saw you breaking her law?" Eden embraced Mr. Shale. She peered into his soulful graying eyes and said, "She would know that you are NOT my slave". Mr. Shale in humility smiled as large as he could and shook his head in agreement.

"Serving you is a joy, princess, and I thank you for saving me." Eden's eyes teared up. "You and I both know the truth. You saved me," she said. Eden flashed back to the moment when Mr. Shale covered her body with his own in an effort to shield her from a soldier's blade during the war when she was a child. That is why Mr. Shale has limited use of his left arm. Eden remarks, "Shall we proceed to the palace?"

Males Are A Threat...

Ilya never wastes a moment to exercise her authority. She knows she is destined to rule. Her entire mindset and demeanor reflect that destiny. In her efforts to lead, she spends her morning meeting with the citadel provost and executives. As one of the environmentalists and physicists complete their presentation, Ilya receives a notice. She purses her lips as her breathing deepens.

The environmental engineer reminds everyone that the males did not destroy all of the natural resources during the war. She states that the forests still holds vast supplies that are at the disposal of the citizens.

Ilya passes the memo to another council member who interrupts the presentation. She flips her long red hair behind her shoulder before she proceeds to read the report placed in her hand. It states that unknown rebel males have been spotted in the forests. "Surely these rebels pose no threat to the advancement of our civilization." Princess Ilya is reassured by one of the military leaders that the rebels will not be a hindrance. She states,

"Our forces are securing the forests as we speak." The officials applaud and the meeting is adjourned.

Princess Ilya commands that a private meeting with her Chief of Security be arranged immediately regarding this situation. She warns, "We must eliminate any threats."

Males Start As Dangerous Infants...

Lliam kisses Elizabeth on the forehead before he places a locket around her neck. He then kisses his son. He places a sack filled with supplies and food across her shoulder before warning them to be careful. "Follow the path to the east wall. You will find a hidden entrance back into the city there," he says. They embrace and say a prayer. Elizabeth is virtually paralyzed before Lliam. She finds it difficult to force her feet to walk away from him. The fear in her blue eyes breaks Lliam. Yet, she finds the strength to depart with their son.

"Go," Lliam commands as he watches Elizabeth's figure becomes smaller in the distance. Lliam begs GOD to watch over them. Then his attention is suddenly diverted when he hears voices. He quickly tries to hide.

Before The Kingdom...

The depth and the currents of the canal off the river is an intimidating barrier that lies between Elizabeth and the citadel. Moreover, the massive iron and stone gates of the citadel proved to be more threatening. She prays fervently to GOD for a way to cross the waters without having to risk swimming across. That is when she finds the remains of a make-shift raft slightly hidden by the overhanging trees at the water's edge.

With the baby wrapped tightly to her, Elizabeth makes her way onto the dilapidated and distressed wooded structure. The beams which were loosely held together with rope still showed signs of function. With a large tree branch in hand, Elizabeth paddles across the canal. Waves of the bitter cold water splash onto the baby causing him to cry. Elizabeth tries to quiet him as they draw closer to shore.

She fears that the cries of the baby will alert the guards. That fear becomes a reality when they are soon surrounded by three females. Elizabeth tries to explain, "I found the infant crying by the water's edge. I assumed he was left to die."

The guards peered at the child. Then, the guards looked at each other.

Elizabeth reassures them that the reason she decided to save him was because she believed that he could be raised to become a domestic slave. This explanation satisfied the guards. They had Elizabeth and the infant escorted inside the citadel and directly to the hospital.

Males Are To Humble Themselves...

"Good morning grandmother", Eden remarks as she and Mr. Shale approach. Mr. Shale bows ever so slowly. "Please forgive me for being so late. I intend no disrespect to you as the queen or as my grandmother," Eden says. The queen looks at Mr. Shale. But Eden redirects her attention towards her grandmother, the queen, and assures her that Mr. Shale did everything he could to awaken her. "I simply failed to get up on time."

Eden kisses her grandmother on the cheek as an act of requesting her forgiveness.

Eden politely refuses to be served breakfast by one of the male slaves. Her grandmother asks if she is feeling well because she noticed that she has been hardly eating. Before Eden can answer, they are interrupted.

Princess Ilya arrives with her less than modest entourage inclusive of Amblin, Vayl, her personal attendant and a commanding officer. She formally greets Eden and their grandmother, the queen. By the polished look of her attire, it is evident that Ilya undoubtedly lives by the royal standard. In her demands for ultimate service and accommodations, Ilya was becoming the strong princess that the queen so desired.

Eden, however, never concerns herself with all the attention that their grandmother would pour over Ilya. Over the years, Eden shied away from it more and more. She concerned herself more with social or civil matters. Nonetheless, Eden's attention is drawn to a report that is brought to the queen.

Males Must Be Registered...

The glare of the morning sun required that the guards wear protective shades. A commanding officer places her hand on the panel. Her fingerprints are confirmed. The monitor is activated. She gives orders. The city gates are opened and several new male captives are escorted inside. They are made to march approximately half a mile through the glass-encased tunnel before they fully enter inside the citadel.

The sunlight made the entire city glow. Every building seemed to be erected of the finest metals encased in heavy pillars of crystal. The pathways were made of flawlessly polished marble with flecks of gold. The greenery of the gardens seemed to mirror the forests outside the perimeter. The only difference was that inside this citadel the aroma of eucalyptus and gardenias was more heavily present. Every structure had large white and gray stone foundation. The mere initial sight of the citadel was beyond blinding and overwhelming.

The new captives seemed confused. As they take in the brilliance of the scene the citadel, they become overwhelmed by their new circumstance. Each of them watched women blissfully pass by while other males bound with thick metal bands around their ankles diligently worked all around them. They were made to stand in a single file line. One by one they approached the medical registrants who obtained their vitals before injecting them with a tranquilizing serum. Few of the captives tried to resist, but they were shocked into compliance.

One captive pleads with a registrant nurse to release him so that he can find his son. She fights back the desire to show the captive mercy because she has been taught that males are incapable of concern. Thus, she orders him to bow. He peers at her with tears. She avoids his gaze so that she can administer the injection. He is instantly rendered unconscious. While the nurse watches the captive fall to the ground, she discreetly wipes away a tear and nods for him to be removed.

The captives are then transported to the diagnostic inspection facility where they receive full neurological, physiological and psychological examinations.

Report of New Captives...

During her meal with the council, Vayl receives a document. "Chief of Security" is labeled onto envelope. Vayl opens and reads before revealing the content to Ilya. "We must go quickly," Ilya says to Vayl. Eden watches as her cousin, Ilya, rises to share the document with the queen. Eden becomes alarmed.

News begins to spread throughout the congregation regarding the new captives. The queen grants Ilya permission to exercise her authority. Ilya and her two blonde allies, Vayl and Amblin, along with her security team depart and proceed to the screening diagnostic facility to investigate.

Eden maintains her seated position next to her grandmother after Ilya and her team departs. Within moments, Eden excuses herself to follow her cousin. She feels obligated to look into the findings.

Males Must Be Screened...

Upon entering the screening room, the new captives were visible through a digital two-way mirror. All the new captives were lying unconscious on steel slabs. There were electrodes and IVs attached to their bodies.

The initial sight of the new captives disturbed Eden once she entered the screening room. Deliberately and quietly, Eden seated herself in a chair located directly behind Ilya and observed the screening process.

The physicians began to post data regarding the new captive inventory onto the monitors. Each captive was stripped, cleansed, scanned, vaccinated, probed, injected, labeled and tagged in a mechanical manner. Eden tried to hide her uneasiness at the sight of the labor-intensive inventory process. She found it to be extremely sterile, calculated, and clinical.

However, Amblin, who was seated adjacent to Ilya, found the process to be most beneficial. Since they were little girls, Eden tried to evade Amblin's manipulative schemes. Eden knew how divisive Amblin's character could be. Yet, she was also aware that even though Amblin was quite the opportunist, she was fairly harmless. Amblin simply enjoyed attention and prestige. Being closely tied to the royal family offered her just that.

Besides, it was clear to Eden that Ilya seemed to enjoy being persuaded by Amblin. She never lacked innovative ways to encourage Ilya to use her authority to forward her agenda. Eden on the other hand did her best to minimize contact.

With the presentation of each new male captive by the physicians, Ilya's entourage were not devoid comments. It was no surprise that Amblin made suggestions as to which captives should be placed in the unit for breeding.

The other women present engaged in making mildly inappropriate and derogatory comments regarding the captives which Eden found awkwardly difficult to tolerate. She refused to participate in their offensiveness.

Instead, Eden found herself wondering how these males were able to care for themselves in the forests. It was hard to envision where they lived all this time. She felt genuine sorrow and concern for them.

As each male was being tagged for inventory, Eden observed their physical conditions from a more concerned perspective. They all had minimal evidence of being shackled. Aside from minor scratches, they seemed to be in good physical condition.

One of the captives immediately captured Eden's attention. He had thick wavy long hair with a more clean-shaven face. Much unlike many of the prior captives and slaves, his fingernails appeared clean and almost manicured with minimal callouses on his palms. He had no signs of scars, tattoos or piercings. Even in his supine position, he seemed lean and tall with strong facial features. Eden wondered if he were possibly educated.

Inventory data that coincided with his tag number was visible on the screen. Eden searched for his personal file.

No violent charges were listed. Eden developed a curious fascination with this captive. Medics continued running their battery of tests on the remaining captives. Soon after, they were dressed in the customary gray servant attire. Princess Ilya allowed Amblin to prepare the recommendations for unit assignments for the captives.

Eden reviewed the units that they were assigned while Ilya drew near. Ilya whispered to Eden, "Don't worry little cousin. I know you are getting up in age. I selected an optimal breeder for you." Eden disturbingly closed her eyes and leaned her head back as Ilya departed. She tried to contain her upset at her cousin's offensive comments. Eden did not follow her cousin out. Instead, she watched the captives being prepared for transport to the containment facility.

Eden allows herself to step inside of the screening room. She was intimidated by the sound of the monitors and the smells of the antiseptics. As the nurses complete their documentation, Eden slowly circles the slab to inspect the captives who are shackled to the table. She purposely approaches the captive who intrigued her.

The screening room begins to empty. "Are you coming, miss?" a nurse asks. Eden nods and watches the nurse depart. As Eden prepares to exit, she feels a grip of cold fingers around her wrist. She turns around in panic to find this captive awake. The stare from his green eyes intimidates her. Yet, she finds a kindness in them. Before she can come to her senses quickly enough to scream, he releases her arm only to be rendered unconscious again.

The nurse calls to Eden once more. "Would you like us to wait for you?" she says. Eden turns to face the nurse.

"Are you okay?" the nurse asks. In an attempt to hide the offensive action of this new male captive physically touching her, Eden simply answers the nurse with a smile and a nod.

Males Are To Avoid Eye Contact...

The new captives get abruptly awakened by a forceful female voice. "Get dressed!" Still disoriented from the effects of the tranquilizer, they begin to stand. One captive attempts to regain his faculties so that he could understand what was happening to him. He scans his surroundings to realize that he is not alone in his confusion. He apparently has a roommate.

The heavy glass doors slide open. Secured in restraints, both males begin to exit their glass containments. The female guards escorted the two new captives to the dining hall. They are seated adjacent to one another. Lliam whispers, "I have to get out of here so that I can find my son." With the guards scrutinizing their every move, Ezekiel resists the desire to look at his newly fellow captive. From the deep sigh and the lowering of his head, Ezekiel senses his upset and defeat.

Ezekiel and Lliam stand at attention while more captives enter the hall. As each new captive passes by, Ezekiel immediately recognizes a scar on the forearm of one of them. Ezekiel recalls where he last saw that scar as he raises his head and locks eyes with the captive. He senses that he is dangerous.

Their eye contact is broken when the Chief of Security begins to speak. She insists that the new captives observe their new surroundings. "Welcome to your new home," Vayl says. As she briefs them on the regulations, Ezekiel's attention is focused on the captive with the scar. He observes how massive in stature he is.

Vayl nears the completion of her speech. She assures the new captives, "As long as you obey and respect women, you will find life within the new order quite fair and pleasant. Vayl bids the slaves well before they are taken to assignment release.

Ezekiel maintains minimal expression before he whispers to his new comrade, "If I am to help you rescue your son, then it would help me if you told me your name." With hope in his voice, he answers, "I'm Lliam".

Males Must Be Assigned...

The mere sound of the heavily armed guards marching in unison made Ezekiel and Lliam nervous. The new captives displayed astonishment at the sight of the multitude of female soldiers standing before them as they entered the auditorium of the male containment facility. Ezekiel questioned the new world he was being forced to live in.

It was far different from the quiet, small and non-hierarchal community he had known. His former world predominately consisted of agriculturists and engineers who were both male and female. When he scanned this room, he did not find one male authority figure present.

Lliam was equally overwhelmed at the number of enslaved males. Lliam was slightly smaller in stature, but quite lean and seemingly intelligent.

Ezekiel whispered, "Where are we?" Lliam replies, "I have no idea, but I know one thing. We had better pray this place does not become our future." The auditorium is constructed of stainless steel walls with a metallic floor. Large telecom screens with glass inserts complete the setting. Every entrance contains an electronic gate with an identification panel.

The new captives slowly become accustomed to arranging themselves into a single file line. One by one, guards electronically scan their hands. The scanning alarms Ezekiel because he realizes that a device must have been inserted in his hand while he was unconscious. He withholds his upset when the guard approaches.

Ezekiel watches as female guards apprehend Lliam and escort him along a corridor with an arrow labeled gate ASSIGNMENT T. His attention gets distracted away from Lliam, when a thick metal bracelet is secured onto his right ankle.

As the wand passes over Ezekiel's skin, the guard informs him that his gate is ASSIGNMENT B. She then instructs Ezekiel to step forward. He hesitates initially, but finally surrenders and complies.

The steel door slides open. Ezekiel along with three other captives are commanded to proceed inside. Ezekiel notices that the rooms are encased inside glass walls which appear to be laboratories. There is a gymnasium with an indoor track and equipment. There is also a nutrition center completed with classrooms.

A large telecom screen, located at the front of the classroom, projects an image of an exotic Asian woman. She begins to speak. "Welcome to Unit B Assignment," she states. The men attentively listen to her instructions. "Located behind you is your required uniform. You will be granted time to change before the guards arrive. Upon their arrival, please bow until they further provide you with instructions. You will be provided with personal supplies and a regulations manual. They will introduce you to your tasks and will serve as guides. You would do well to heed their every command. Please do not resist. It is in your best interest to embrace your new role in our society," she says. The screen turns off.

The four males stare at each other in confusion and silence. A series of beeps are heard before the steel door slides open. Female guards armed heavily in military gear flood the classroom. They surround the new captives. Each male slowly dropped to his knees to bow. Ezekiel stares mindlessly at their boots as one guard issues a command. He is in disbelief.

Facing Her Reality...

"I see that you're still afraid of needles. Some things never change," the nurse says as she watches Eden's eyes grow wide. She instructs Eden to close her eyes and take a deep breath. While Eden breathes, the nurse states, "We are done." Eden expresses relief at the fact that she did not feel a thing. The nurse simply smiles while she collects the vials of blood. "Dr. Delaney will be with you shortly," the nurse says as she exits.

Eden anxiously stares at the various illustrations of the female anatomy posted throughout the exam room. She is drawn to the anatomical model of a baby in-utero. She traces the outline of the baby with her index finger.

Suddenly, the door slides opens. Dr. Delaney enters with her hair clipped atop her head and wearing her distinguished white lab coat. As Eden watches Dr. Delaney wrinkle her nose in an effort to squint at her chart, she always found Dr. Delaney to be full of sage advice and hopeful solutions. She greets Eden with a hug. "Glad I didn't have to have a guard drag you in here," Dr. Delaney laughs. "How are you"? Eden states she is fine, but Dr. Delaney is not convinced.

"Eden we grew up together. I know when you are telling a lie". Eden is hesitant about sharing with Dr. Delaney her feelings of sadness and emptiness. She silently looks at the anatomical model on the counter that she was just handling. Dr. Delaney follows Eden's line of sight and says, "I think I may understand now."

Dr. Delaney activates the computerized chart. After reviewing the vitals, Dr. Delaney asks Eden to answer honestly. "Would you like to have a baby?" Eden cautiously makes eye contact.

When it comes to Eden defending herself, she always had a difficult time. Unlike Ilya, Eden struggled throughout the years to state what she feels because she suffered a type of survivor's guilt ever since the war ended. It did not help that Eden also grew up with a cousin who constantly reminded her of her inadequacies. Eden had to maintain integrity, strength and dignity in the presence of the royals in order to overcome criticisms.

As Eden attempts to gather her thoughts and words, Dr. Delaney tries to ease her struggle. In an effort to provide comfort, Dr. Delaney respectfully fills in the answers. She lowers her voice and reaches to hold Eden's hand. Dr. Delaney says, "You fear that at your somewhat mature age you may NOT be able to have a baby, right?" Tears roll down Eden's cheek. Dr. Delaney looks Eden in the eyes and insists that there is no need for her to worry. "Thanks to your grandmother, our queen, nothing is impossible in our new world. Please remember that," Dr. Delaney declares.

Males Issued Cellmates...

Ezekiel follows his fellow captives down the corridor. They approach an enclosed glass cubicle complete with beds, disposal facilities, a computerized screen, a desk, chairs and ventilation holes. The guard activates the panel which opens the sliding glass door. The first captive is asked to enter. The door slides shut.

They continue down the corridor. Two more captives are placed in their glass cells. They approach the last glass cubicle. Ezekiel sees a much older gentleman inside sitting at the desk. Ezekiel is ordered to enter by an armed guard who then activates the heavy glass door to slide closed behind him.

The older white-haired gentleman turns around, removes his glasses and with boldness extends his right hand. He introduces himself to Ezekiel.

"I am Pastor Eli". In hesitation, Ezekiel stares at his outstretched hand before he shakes it. "Nice to meet you under these rather unorthodox circumstances," Pastor Eli says. Ezekiel takes a deep breath.

"It's been a long time since the women introduced new captives to the order," says Pastor Eli. Ezekiel frowns up his forehead in alarm. He continues to listen to the pastor. "They must have recognized something very special in you to have assigned you to this unit. Either you are especially educated, especially gifted or an especially huge threat," Pastor Eli suggests.

Ezekiel asks, "What is this place? What has happened to all the men? Why are they holding us here?" Pastor Eli senses his frustrations.

"Oh son, where would I dare to start? Well, to answer your most essential question, you and I have become slaves here in their world, according to their laws," Pastor Eli states. Ezekiel stares expressionless and in disbelief.

Pastor Eli remarks, "By the look on your face, I sense that none of this is making any sense." Ezekiel is silent.

Pastor Eli attempts to provide an alternative explanation. "When the war ended, all males were forced into slavery. I have been enslaved here for the past thirty-plus years of my life and it is hard for even me to absorb all of this."

Ezekiel asks, "Why? What did the men do? How did women find the power to enslave all of the men? How were they able to create such a society? That seems virtually impossible to conceive."

Pastor Eli replies, "I know that you ask these questions with great concern, but you should ask these questions with great humility. Like most men, you underestimate the power of these women. You see every woman as a weaker vessel. Yet, these women have the ability to operate as a collective force that could easily overpower any male. As that collective force, they recognized the brutality of the men. And as that collective force, they decided to put an end to the destructive impact of men."

Ezekiel still seemed uncertain about the information Pastor Eli shared. He could not make sense of what compelled the women to establish such a powerful society. Ezekiel was born after the war. He had only heard of the war. However, he had grown up far removed from the territory where the war had occurred.

All that Ezekiel had known of males was exemplified in his cousins, his uncles and especially his father. He never witnessed any of them exercising any brutal behavior towards women. This news left him speechless.

While trying to absorb this information, Ezekiel closes his eyes and recalls a memory with his parents before his father passed away. He remembers the day his father brought him a puppy. At the sight of the animal, his mother instantly shook her head in complete upset. No sooner could his mother continue her argument, his father surprised his mother with her favorite flowers. It was hard for her to contain her anger in that moment, but she certainly tried.

Pastor Eli continues, "I guess you could say that this entire new world was established by the women out of the exact same fear and violence created by the men that they sought to eliminate. During the war, the women and children truly suffered various trials and tragedies, even death. Any form of torment that came to the mind of men was imparted unmercifully upon the women and children. The men had broken them all."

"Once the men stopped being fathers, brothers, husbands, providers, comforters, teachers, supporters, mentors, leaders and protectors, they became the true enemy to all women. This female ruled society is the result of the sins of every man. The women sought to completely protect themselves from anything that has a hint of male domination. This would include even the plan GOD has for all mankind," Pastor Eli says.

Ezekiel remains stunned over Pastor Eli's words because he could never imagine harming the one woman he adored most, his mother. In that moment, he flashes back to a day when he arrived home from school to find his mother fervently packing. She offered him little explanation. Yet, he could overhear his uncle warning his mother to protect her son.

Ezekiel returns to his senses when he hears voices calling out, "Dad, are you okay?" Pastor Eli reassures them that he is fine. Pastor Eli apologizes to Ezekiel for the outbursts. "Those are my sons, EJ and Emil." Then, Pastor Eli answers, "Gentlemen, I was speaking to our new arrival. I failed to get your name."

"I am Ezekiel."

Encounter With An Unusual Male...

The sun glares through the sliding glass doors of the hospital. Eden is relieved to see the exit. However, she gets distracted by the sign labeled "Infant Containment Units". Pausing short of exiting the facility, she begins to follow the marked arrows.

She inches along the corridor until she reaches the units. There is a distinction between the infant units. The unit for the females was nothing short of luxury, but for the males not so much.

Eden could smell the sweet fragrance that lingered from the female infant containment unit. Yet, a cry drew Eden further along the corridor to the infant male containment unit. She peered through the observation glass. The room appeared cold and sterile. Every inch of the floor, walls and furnishings were made of steel or glass.

Eden observes a woman carefully cradling one of the male infants. This captivates Eden. She notices that the woman is not dressed in the uniform required of medical staff. Eden finds her to be stunning in appearance with her long dark hair and piercing blue eyes.

The woman looks around as if to see if anyone is watching her. Eden quickly hides from the woman's view. After a few minutes, Eden peeks out to continue observing the woman.

Eden is confused at why this woman seems to be showing so much concern for this infant. As the woman paces the floor, she begins to sing to the baby. Eden notices a distinct birthmark on the bottom of the infant's right foot. It strongly resembles that of a spike.

Suddenly, someone calls Eden's name. The woman holding the infant inside the unit also seems to hear because she panics. Eden turns to find the voice of the woman calling out to her and tries to run interference.

Eden realizes that the woman calling out to her is a friend of Ilya named Sage. She greets Eden with a hug. Sage is an engineer who commands attention with her tall frame. She exclaims, "It's so good to see you. Are you on your way to the trial? Ilya mentioned that the slave could face execution." Eden is speechless at this news.

As Eden tries to absorb the information, she remembers the women she was observing. Thus, she looks back into the infant male unit to find the woman missing. Sage states, "Why don't you come with me? We can catch up on our way to the arena." Eden decides to accompany Sage to the trial.

Males Are Subject To Public Trial...

Alarms begin to sound. Everyone in the citadel is alerted to proceed towards the arena. Even the male slaves get escorted. Ezekiel is forced to attend in his restraints. He inquires of Pastor Eli as to what is happening.

Once the new captives enter into the arena, Ezekiel is overwhelmed at the enormity of the crowd. Seeing so many males shackled together on a gravel-covered area of the arena floor troubles Ezekiel. The area is marked as reserved for slaves and he soon joins them there.

With walls seemingly constructed of metal and concrete, they extended virtually into the sky. The concentric shape of the facility allowed for optimal viewing throughout the stadium, especially the throne area reserved for the royals and such dignitaries. They were seated high above the arena floor as well as the platform.

The applause and the cheers become thunderous when the queen arises from the throne above and waves to those below. Predictably, Princess Ilya positions herself adjacent her grandmother, the queen.

Between the colorful sights of the banners and the refreshing scent coming from the citrus trees dominate the atmosphere inside the arena. Every judge and dignitary is acknowledged before the crowd as they are carefully led up the steps onto the massive platform. A member of the royal council stands to address the women of the citadel regarding the charges against a slave. Sage and Eden arrive in time to watch the slave get escorted to the platform.

The attorneys who were dressed in long royal red robes begin presenting the case before the presiding judges of the court. As the charges are being read, Ezekiel spots Lliam in the midst. He notices the different assignment letters placed on the prisoners. He asks Pastor Eli seated next to him to explain what the letters represent. Pastor Eli explains that the letters represent the categorical assignments for which the women would find a particular male to be useful. "For instance, a male who is assigned to the D unit represents the Domestic inventory," says Pastor Eli. Ezekiel awaited further explanation.

Pastor Eli then says, "Thus, an assignment to the F unit would represent farming. The E unit represents all levels of engineering. The R unit which was my original unit stands for religion. The C unit means the male will work construction. If you had been placed on the M unit then you would be performing mechanical work. The T unit is for technology." As soon as Pastor Eli made that statement, Ezekiel recalled his new friend, Lliam, being escorted there.

The commissioner of the court stands to address the crowd. As she speaks, Ezekiel returns his attention again to Pastor Eli to inquire about the representation of their unit. Pastor Eli took a deep breath before he makes a statement. "The women have found you and my sons to be superior specimen in terms of intelligence, genetic health, strength, temperament, morality, skills, talent, stature and appearance. That is why you have been selected for breeding."

Ezekiel is troubled. He asks, "How did they make such a determination regarding any of our traits?"

Pastor Eli tries to offer an explanation. "When you were being processed, every type of medical, neurological and genetic tests was being performed on you. These women also have access to any records you may have. From your retinal identification marker alone, they were probably able to determine who you are, where you are from and what kind of person you are," Pastor Eli says.

They return their focus to the slave on the platform. Charges of physical assault are read against him. The prosecuting attorney requests that the judges impose a harsh sentence since his crime was committed against a woman. Everyone reacts to this recommendation.

Eden and Sage are finally able to join the crowd of onlookers. Eden intently observes the face of the prisoner. His appearance is rough. Yet, his head and eyes are tilted up to the sky as if he is searching for a merciful reprieve. She also observes the reaction of the women to the statement from her specific vantage view in the crowd. Yet, Ezekiel watches the men's reaction from his view on bended knee of the arena floor.

Eden suddenly recalls her dream with the angel and she becomes desperate. She knows that she must stop these proceedings. That is when she makes her attempt to push through the crowd during the commotion.

Meanwhile, the prosecution makes arguments as to why this prisoner deserves a minimal sentence of amputation. However, Eden who, is out of breath, finally reaches the bench. Her cousin is surprised at her appearance during these court proceedings because Eden does not usually participate in political or legal activities. Moreover, Ilya finds her presence unusual because she knows that Eden gets easily overwhelmed and timid. Nonetheless, everyone await Eden's actions with anticipation.

Winded and coughing, Eden nervously speaks. "With all due respect, these proceedings are questionable. We have no proof as to what transpired? Where is the victim? Where is her statement? We cannot judge even a male based on hearsay. If you want to impose a harsh sentence then indisputable evidence is required."

Eden's statement stirs the crowd. Yet, her words impress Ezekiel. One judge orders the court to be silent. Eden continues to try and catch her breath. After the judges talk among themselves, they concur that what Eden has presented is valid. Thus, they postpone the proceedings.

The male slaves express unanimous relief. The prisoner lowers his head as if in gratitude. Eden notices her personal servant, Mr. Shale, smiling in approval at her actions. Pastor Eli in humility turns to Ezekiel and says, "Son, GOD sent you here to save all of us including that woman on the platform." Pastor Eli looks towards Eden while speaking still to Ezekiel, "This institution of slavery is in no way your fault, but it has definitely become your problem."

Males Are Forbidden to Meet ...

A food tray is placed on the table next to Ezekiel. He withholds his glance. "Is someone sitting here?" a familiar voice asks. He looks up to see Lliam standing next to him in the feeding station. They exchanged brief smiles as Lliam sits. Utensils could be heard striking plates. Pastor Eli keeps the dialog to a whisper below the noise of the utensils during the meal.

His sons and other slaves at the table listen attentively as he speaks at the level of a whisper. Pastor Eli says, "Women by nature should never be so heartless and ruthless. It goes against GOD. Some of you have been enslaved here more than half of your lives. Have any of you ever once thought about how you inherited this life of slavery? Do you care?" Pastor Eli tries to guide their thoughts.

Pastor Eli continues, "We have been enslaved by women, who for all intensive purposes are supposed to be our sisters, our mothers, our daughters, our wives and our best friends. Instead, we have become their sole enemy. This did not happen because they hate us. This happened because they fear us. This social condition was decades and even centuries in the making. And this last war did not create this current world. Every war since the beginning of time collectively did." The men who are at a loss for words continue to listen to Pastor Eli speak.

"It was every raised voice, unkind word or abusive tone spoken against the women. It was every act of aggression, every fist and every form of disrespect. Every time their cries fell upon deaf ears and their tears were purposely ignored, it built another link in our chains. Sin and selfishness had become so contagious that its impact intensified with every generation of men. These problems started before any of us were ever born. Nevertheless, it is up to us to right these wrongs, before this life of slavery becomes our permanent future."

Lliam clears his throat and affirms, "I must save my son from this life. My son will not become a monster, despite what these women believe. He is no future threat."

Ezekiel places his utensil on the table and as he carefully chooses how to address this question to Lliam. "How do you know that your son won't become a monster?" Ezekiel's question catches everyone off guard. Lliam exclaims, "What are you saying?"

Ezekiel raises his head and reiterates. "What if the women aren't entirely wrong? How do you know that your son will not become a monster like the men who killed my mother?"

The tension at the table begins to rise in the midst of silence. Yet, it is quickly broken when a guard walks by. Lliam appears paralyzed in his attempt to respond. After a long pause Lliam humbly states, "He is my son. I am his father. I know that the same spirit that lies within me lies inside of him. He is not a monster."

Lliam and Ezekiel stare at each other intensely as if they were seeking understanding from one another. Pastor Eli redirects their focus and says in confirmation, "Only an honorable man can raise another honorable man. This I know." Then, he looks at his two sons in admiration.

The men in that moment seem begin to bond. That is when Emil who is the elder son of Pastor Eli says, "Dad is right. We must restore their trust in us. And no offense gentlemen, I personally don't want to spend the rest of my life waking up to any of you. I want to wake up next to one of them." They laugh discretely.

EJ, Pastor Eli's youngest son, asks, "Are we talking about planning an escape?" They await an answer.

"You will need to do more than plan an escape. You will need to find a way to bring about a change of their hearts and minds. And I highly suggest you start at the top. There seems to be one woman who is concerned with our well-being so much so that she single-handedly stopped the execution of one of our own today. For the first time since the war, a woman defended one of us. And this woman happens to live in the palace," he recalls.

Facing Disgruntled Family...

Eden is startled by the slam of the door. She turns to find Ilya staring at her. With the redness in her cheeks matching the fire in her hair, Ilya asks in anger, "What is wrong with you? I cannot believe you defended a male. Why would you do that? Don't you have anything to say miss future attorney? You had plenty to say in that slave's defense," Ilya yells.

Suddenly, Ilya calms her hostility and continues to speak. "Do you have any idea what kind of message you are sending? They are males. They are worse than animals. They are a dangerous sub-species," she reminds.

"When they commit crimes, we don't question the reasons for their behaviors. We don't seek to understand them. And we certainly don't dare extend mercy to them, because they are males. They have repeatedly proven throughout history that they cannot be trusted not to inflict harm on humanity. Was there a reason you decided to grand stand on that stage today? Did you enjoy embarrassing our family?" Ilya asks.

Eden puts her head down in shame before she says, "It felt wrong to allow him to suffer." Eden struggled to find the right words to say. All she could do was recall the angel in her dream warning her to not allow the shedding of innocent blood. Yet, Eden could not tell Ilya that her actions were encouraged by a warning from a dream.

Ilya walks toward Eden and cradles her face in her hands. Ilya says, "Eden, right now all of the women including grandmother think you are out of your mind. But, it is no secret how caring your heart is. That is probably why grandmother couldn't allow you to ever become a ruler. Although we love your tender heart, it does cloud your decision-making." Ilya continues, "I am sorry for being harsh with you. I actually should be thanking you for reminding me of what mercy actually looks like. I guess it would not hurt to extend mercy to the slaves at times."

"Please cousin, remember. Don't ever lose sight of their true nature. Otherwise, they will begin to mistake your kindness for a weakness." Ilya embraces Eden tenderly before she departs. Mr. Shale overhears every word and is very much disturbed by Ilya.

Afraid To Sleep...

The glare from the clock lights the ceiling. Eden sees that the time is 3:35am. She is frustrated. She simply cannot sleep. She is fearful to close her eyes because of that dream. Sitting upright in her bed, she looks out toward the balcony. She decides to get dressed because and take a walk.

Under the darkness of the sky, she can hear the faint sounds of insects in the breeze. She walks to the arena and sits in one of the seats that had been reserved for the male slaves. The concrete bench feels cold and uncomfortable. She wonders how the males could bare to sit there. She stares at the stage until the dawn peaks. Before long, Eden finds herself back at the observation window at the infant male containment unit.

Eden leans her forehead against the glass. Memories of her past childhood flood her mind. A nurse enters the male unit. She checks the monitors on the incubators and she adjusts their IVs. She smiles at Eden and exits. Eden quietly prepares to leave when she sees the woman who disappeared yesterday. Eden strongly suspects that this woman is NOT part of the hospital staff.

The woman nervously looks around as if she were making sure that she was alone. She picks up the infant with the distinct birthmark on his right foot. She places her hand on his forehead and begins to pray.

Eden walks carefully inside as not to startle the woman. She cautiously approaches the woman from behind. Elizabeth realizes that she is no longer alone. She slowly turns around and faces Eden. They stare at one another in silence. As Eden stares at the woman's blue eyes, she senses that this woman is deeply afraid when she sees her hands trembling.

Before Eden can speak, the doors slide open behind her. A nurse asks abruptly who the two women are. Eden has her back to the nurse. She turns to face the nurse. Instantly, the nurse recognizes Eden. The nurse immediately lowers her head to bow and pleads, "I sincerely apologize. I failed to recognize you from behind." Eden gracefully extends forgiveness.

Eden turns her attention back towards the woman holding the infant. She explains to the nurse that her grandmother provided her with an advisor who has been educating her on recognizable genetic traits in the infant male. The nurse apologizes for the interruption and with permission quickly exits the unit.

Elizabeth is still too afraid to open her mouth to say thank you. Eden asks, "Do you know who I am?" Elizabeth humbly shakes her head no. Eden asks, "Would you mind telling me who you are?"

"My name is Elizabeth."

Eden looks at the child and asks, "Would you please tell me who he is?" Elizabeth looks down at the baby and says, "He is my son."

Males Are Not Allowed To Pray...

The sun breaks through the window of their cell bringing so much warmth. Pastor Eli bows down and humbles himself in prayer before the rays of light. Ezekiel approaches and joins Pastor Eli. They smile at each other and Pastor Eli begins, "Have mercy on your servants Lord. Please fill us with your wisdom, favor, mercy and courage and allow us to restore healing, peace and hope to this land."

Their prayer is abruptly interrupted when they hear EJ's voice calling. Ezekiel thinks to himself how much EJ's deep voice does not match his short stature. Very much unlike his brother, Emil, EJ is short. "Dad, we will all be ready. We know what must be done."

Following breakfast, a few of the slaves from the Breeding Unit are escorted to the hospital lab for genetic testing. Ezekiel, EJ and Emile are included in the schedule. Emil and his younger brother, EJ, are familiar with the design of hospital and its proximity to the gates of the citadel because they helped to design the underground passage ways into the hospital facility. EJ had engineering training prior to the war. They share the routes with Ezekiel so that he can have them memorized.

Males Should Be Allowed Legal Defense...

Every whisper, every conversation and every question regarding Eden's actions at the trial filled the royal dining hall that morning. Even the male slaves who were positioned to attend to the needs of the royals discretely focused the various discussions among the council.

These women were bold in their criticisms of Eden. With the queen absent, Eden's actions were without defense. However, Eden was not without an ally because her beloved Mr. Shale was very much present and attentive.

Inside The Queen's Quarters...

Ilya requests to enter her grandmother's quarters. Once inside, she greets her grandmother with a kiss. Ilya knows that her grandmother governs unapologetically and powerfully. However, she is very much aware of the impact that Eden has on their grandmother. Eden can weaken her grandmother's stance on any issue and Ilya cannot contend.

Ilya approaches her grandmother with the hope that she can have a similar effect with her words. As she bows she respectfully addresses her grandmother. "Pardon me grandmother for the interruption. I felt it was vital to discuss the matter of the trial privately away from the council. I trust that you have already spoken with Eden regarding her actions."

The queen turns towards Ilya and says, "It was not necessary for me to address Eden primarily since you have already asserted your authority regarding the matter." Ilya looked at her grandmother in shock.

Her grandmother continued, "Why do you look so surprised? You should know that nothing gets past me. I am fully aware of every harsh word that you spoke against your cousin." At these words, Ilya tries to hide her embarrassment with indignant anger. While her grandmother is speaking, Ilya assumes that Eden had informed their grandmother of what was spoken. Ilya asks, "What did she tell you?"

Her grandmother provides no direct answer. Instead, she states the following, "Ilya, you are like me in virtually every way. I would often tell myself how proud I was of that fact because that meant you were strong like me. But I think I have to blame myself for raising you too strong. Clearly, I failed to fill you with mercy because you had none to give, not even to your own family. I cannot allow you to become harsh and unreasonable like that in regards to the justice of anyone including the males." Ilya burned silently with rage.

The queen continued, "I agree that your cousin approached the court in an unorthodox manner. She did fail to follow protocol. However, she is to be commended for acknowledging the human rights of everyone. This would include the slaves because they are humans as well. The questions she posed prevented us from becoming unjust and brutal like the males. She showed great courage by confronting the court. We all needed to be awakened and challenged."

Ilya hides her frustration behind a smile. She refuses to let her grandmother sense her jealousy of Eden.

Males Are Not To Be Protected...

The male infant sleeps soundly in Elizabeth's arms. Eden approaches and carefully folds back the corner of the blanket to reveal the softness of his face. Eden becomes overwhelmed at the sight of watching him breathe. She places her hand gently on his chest. Elizabeth watches.

"You gave birth to this male?" Eden asks with subtle authority. While still unaware of Eden's identity, Elizabeth fears Eden will turn her into the guards. She knows the inevitable fate of males in this civilization. All she can do is focus on protecting her son. Eden places the blanket back in its position and lowers her head.

With a quiver in her voice, Elizabeth gathers enough bravery to plead with Eden to help her save her son. Eden is shocked by the courage of this woman to make such a request. Eden recalls the law which forbids any such aid to a male. Eden knows this all too well since her grandmother mandated this law. Ignorant of this knowledge, Elizabeth continues in her request.

"I know that the women in this kingdom believe that all males are dangerous from birth, but this is my son. He is no threat. I can raise him to be an amazing and loving son who will do more than merely protect women. His father and I can and will raise him to respect and love them as equals." Eden is startled at Elizabeth's announcement of the child having a father. "Did you say 'his father'?"

Veil Of Escape...

Upon entering the lab, the electronic restraints disband thus releasing the slaves. The scent of rubbing alcohol and the sounds of monitors fill the room.

The males remained in their single file line anxiously awaiting instructions. The steel doors slid open allowing two nurses to enter. Each slave was assigned to an exam room. Ezekiel watched one of the nurses enter a code on the exterior wall panel. He attempted to memorize the code before he was instructed to walk inside. The examination room was cold and sterile.

Cautiously, Ezekiel walked towards the stainless steel table where he finds a folded disposable gown. The nurse directs, "Please disrobe and put on the gown. The doctor will be with you shortly." She exits the room to grant Ezekiel privacy.

While undressing, Ezekiel notices that there are no windows in the room. He sees a monitor with his name highlighted. He moved closer to the screen. That is when he noticed the covered metal tray. He lifts the lid only to see a syringe and vials of medicaments. He began to sweat profusely with nervousness. He had no idea what these women were planning. He bowed his head in prayer in order to calm himself. Yet, his prayer was interrupted with a series of beeps which indicated that someone was entering. Ezekiel was almost too nervous to look up because he had not yet followed the instructions to put on the hospital gown.

A deep male voice speaks, "There's no turning back now." The sound of that voice came as a relief because Ezekiel knew exactly who it was before he lifted his head. Lliam commands, "Come! We must hurry and find the others." Ezekiel was all too eager to follow.

Ezekiel remembered that Lliam had been assigned to the Technology Unit. He forgot that Lliam had been skilled in science and engineering.

Lliam leads the way to where he believes the other males are contained. Ezekiel is able to provide Lliam with the clearance code that he previously memorized. Once released, Emil in his enormously tall and stature is able to assure the other males that he can lead them out of the citadel. However, Lliam refuses to leave without his son. Thus, the men decide to split up in order to lessen their chances of being recaptured.

Eden Encounters Escaped Slaves...

Elizabeth continues to await an answer from an all-too-silent Eden. While still in shock, she hides her reaction at Elizabeth's bold request to save her son. As much as Eden was impressed with Elizabeth's courage, she could never even consider helping to rescue a slave, even if that slave was an infant. This request disturbed Eden's consciousness. It was clear that Elizabeth had no idea of Eden's true identity.

Careful to respond, Eden plays with the silence as she slowly encircles Elizabeth. Eden stops and locks eyes with Elizabeth as if she were searching for truth. Within seconds, their stare gets interrupted by the opening of the unit door. Eden is seized with fear when two male slaves run through the door. Elizabeth cries out, "Lliam!" They embrace. Elizabeth starts to cry.

Ezekiel warns them that there is no time for them to have a prolonged reunion. They must get the boy and leave. Ezekiel ceases his orders when he sees Eden. Although he recognizes her from the trial proceedings, he feels as though he has seen her before.

Ezekiel becomes nervous. He looks intently at her. He then asks both Elizabeth and Lliam if they know who she is. They all stare at her. Lliam moves closer in proximity to Elizabeth and Ezekiel. Lliam believes, "Whoever she is, she must be extremely important. Look at the way she is dressed. She is definitely not a worker. She must be pretty valuable among the women in this society."

All of a sudden Elizabeth remembers the encounter from earlier with the nurse. Elizabeth moves closer to Eden and orders, "Wait! That nurse bowed before you as if she feared you." The baby still in Elizabeth's arms begins to awaken drawing everyone's attention away from Eden. Lliam reaches to hold him.

Eden watches in nervousness. Nevertheless, she realizes in that moment that she may be able to escape. She slowly tries to retreat unnoticed from all of them.

That is when Lliam speaks. "Maybe she is one of their royals." They all look at her again. "We have no choice. We must take her with us."

At those words, Eden musters enough courage to make an attempt to escape. She quickly makes a mad dash towards the door, but Ezekiel reacts. He seizes Eden. However, the force and momentum at which he grabs her causes them to both fall. The fall causes Eden to strike her head onto the floor knocking her unconscious.

Ezekiel panics and tries to awaken her. He picks her up in his arms and checks her breathing. Elizabeth tries to help him revive her. "She's still breathing," Ezekiel says. Elizabeth urges them to leave before the guards come. Lliam stubbornly makes it clear that he refuses to leave without her and their son.

Elizabeth reaches for Lliam's face and urges, "The baby needs to remain in this facility for now. They can better care for him and right now he needs any medical attention that these women can provide." They both look at their son. Lliam nods in understanding.

Elizabeth reassures "GOD will provide a way for them to all escape safely. Right now, our son needs the best in medications and nutrition. These women can offer this. I promise to stay close by him and keep him safe. No one is aware that I am not a female citizen of this kingdom," Elizabeth says. Lliam hugs her and the baby tightly.

He whispers in her ear. "I promise to stay nearby to watch over you both. I think I know where I can hide."

She instructs Lliam to help Ezekiel carry Eden's unconscious body out of the citadel.

Definition Of Family...

"You act like Eden is your arch enemy. She is family," Amblin reminds Ilya in her slightly high-pitched voice. Yet, Ilya maintains her focus on the bull's eye and releases her arrow. Armed guards are strategically positioned along the archery field. Ilya selects another arrow from her arsenal. Amblin remains silent to allow Ilya to focus her aim.

She then continues to reason, "Do you feel threatened by your own cousin, because there is no need? Eden admires you tremendously." Ilya provides no response. Amblin then reminds Ilya, "Have you forgotten that you were selected to be the next ruler?"

Ilya releases another arrow from her bow. She seemed unphased at Amblin's statements. Ilya stares off into the direction that the arrow traveled. She inhales deeply and replies, "Amblin you know that you have been a part of our family since we were toddlers." Amblin smiles in response. "We endured tremendous trials. You and I were the ones who protected not only our families, but every woman we could. We took the greatest risks. Yet, we endured even greater losses. Our loved ones were killed. Your mother was murdered. You almost died. We witnessed all the pain. Even though Eden's mother passed during the war, Eden never truly suffered like we did." At this reminder, Amblin's eyes fill with tears.

Ilya turns, faces Amblin and confesses, "You have been more of a sister to me than Eden has ever been. You are beyond loyal. I trust you with my life." Amblin is so broken by these words that she tearfully assures Ilya of her loyalty. They hug. Amblin cherishes this moment with Ilya as they reaffirm the strength of their bond.

Ilya turns away from Amblin to collect herself. Little time passes before the sentiment of their conversation changes. To Amblin's surprise, Ilya inquires, "Which of the new captives seem most ruthless and dangerous?" With her eyebrows raised, Amblin is suddenly at a loss as to how to respond.

Unexpected Kidnapping...

Lliam wipes the sweat from his brow as he struggles to help Ezekiel carry Eden's unconscious body discretely from the hospital to the edge of the citadel gate. The transport of her body proves difficult because they must be careful not to alert the guards or cause her further injury during the hidden five-plus mile walk. They place her body down briefly in order to rest. Lliam instructs Ezekiel how to bypass the secured perimeter. "You must travel north of the northeast corner into the forest. Once you arrive at a clearing, look for a break in between the pines. Amidst the brush, there will be a path. That path will take you to a small wooden cottage which Elizabeth and I once called home. You will be safe there."

Lliam insistes, "I must stay and help the other slaves. And I must save Elizabeth and my son. You understand."

Ezekiel catches his breath enough to hug Lliam. He says, "I completely understand." Before Ezekiel picks up Eden's body again, he confesses, "I have never had a brother until now."

They smile. Lliam teases, "Think of the unnecessary sibling rivalry we managed to avoid." Ezekiel guarantees his imminent trust and return with a smile. They depart.

Report Of Escape...

Ilya hastens to the private quarters of the queen. Many are gathered there before her grandmother. Ilya approaches to see the document in her grandmother's hand. Ilya asks, "Are the reports true?"

Her grandmother hesitantly responds, "I am afraid so."

Instantly, her grandmother began to operate in her role. "I must know who escaped and if there were any injuries," her grandmother commanded. The queen then orders Ilya, "Please have security locate your cousin. She seems to be missing."

Following that order, the queen departs. She leaves Ilya and the council behind to engage further discussion regarding the escape. However, Ilya is further rendered speechless when Vayl whispers additional news in her ear. She hands a document to Ilya that states a slave may have possibly escaped with a female.

Ilya tries to contain her upset by calmly asking Vayl, "Is anyone else aware of this?" Vayl shakes her head. Ilya resumes, "Under no circumstances is this to be reported to anyone else, especially the queen. Do you understand?" Vayl nervously nods.

Ilya suspects that slaves who escaped have possibly taken Eden. As she returns her attention to Vayl, Ilya explains, "We must alert the queen that Eden has become engaged in an engineering water project with her team. It has required her to travel outside the citadel." Vayl agrees while Ilya discards the report in the disposal.

As soon as everyone departs, Mr. Shale makes his way to the disposal container and retrieves the report.

On The Run...

The sun starts to descend as Ezekiel arrives at the clearing. He gently places the unconscious Eden on the ground. His breathing is slightly labored. He wipes sweat from his forehead and stands upright in order to stretch his back and to scan the area.

He starts to talk aloud to GOD. "I seriously need your help here with her." Ezekiel catches his breath and bends over. "You are a whole lot heavier than you actually look." He picks her body up and continues his search for the path of which Lliam told him.

Rebels Recruited By Royalty...

Vayl depresses the button on the intercom. She instructs her soldiers to escort the slaves into the observation hall. On the other side of the two-way digital mirrored glass partition stands Princess Ilya, Vayl and Amblin. They remain awkwardly silent. Amblin breaks the silence with a question. "Are you sure you want to do this?" Before Ilya can answer, the steel door slides open. Three slaves enter the quarantined room while bound in restraints.

They are all distinctly intimidating in stature and rough in appearance. One slave has a distinct scar on his forearm. Yet, all three possess a merciless gaze in their eyes. The telecom monitor begins to display their information. The biographical scan on Nealon downloads. An officer confirms, "These are the slaves that you requested princess." Ilya thanks her and dismisses her.

Amblin reviews the biographical backgrounds of the slaves. "Nealon, age 34, white male, education limited, no living relatives, charged with murder but never convicted.

His fellow playmates, Milam and Stone, apparently grew up with him in a children's shelter. They seemed to be fully equipped with the ruthlessness that you are seeking. I just hope that you know what you are doing. I especially hope your remember that males can never be trusted," Amblin states.

Finding Shelter...

The interior is dark, but the light from the moon shines through the window. It allows Ezekiel to find the bed. He wastes no time in laying Eden's body down. He leaves her bedside in order to search for any medicine that could reduce her swelling of the hematoma on the back of her head. The blow she sustained when they fell at the hospital was significant enough to render her unconscious.

He tries to recall some of the procedures his mother used to perform as a nurse. His hands tremble from exhaustion and nervousness. Yet, he manages to find and open a bottle of analgesics that had a past due expiration. He begins to crush them and pour the crumbled fragments of the pills into her mouth.

"GOD please let her wake up. Please do not let her die," he begs aloud before he lays her back down. "What was I thinking, GOD? Only I would be stupid enough to take this injured woman away from the hospital. Oh GOD, I must get her back there. She needs help," Ezekiel cries as he feels himself becoming overwhelmed with exhaustion. "GOD please help both of us!"

He moves towards a sink to rinse his face. He becomes more aware of the coolness of the room, thus he looks back at her. He returns to her bedside to cover her. He studies her face in the dimness of the light before exhaustion overtakes him. Instantly, he falls asleep.

Males Are Not To Think...

Nealon, Milam and Stone drop to their knees and lower their heads before Princess Ilya and her entourage. In their presence, she wraps her long red hair into a bun before she begins to speak, "We have reviewed your files. You are all notorious for your violent crimes. You all especially seem to be quite skilled in wreaking havoc and inflicting pain on innocent persons, especially women and children." The slaves continue to bow in silence.

"I assume that you all knew each other before your arrival here. Please know that in our society males such as you are executed simply because you have no mercy, no compassion and no concern for human life. It is even more evident that you lack the capacity to change for the better. Thus, you prove to be of no use in our society. However, there is one job that would be useful for your particular level of callousness," Ilya hints.

Awaken to Confusion...

She tries to awaken herself by rubbing her eyes. The rays from the sun are blinding. She squints to focus, but her vision remains blurred. The room seems to spin as she tries to sit up. She feels dizzy. Thus, she places her head back onto the bed and closes her eyes. She tries to figure out where she is and how she got here. She slowly turns her head to find a slave lying on the floor. He appears to be sleeping.

She is startled at the initial sight of him because she does not recognize him. Her frustration intensifies as she struggles to remember what happened. She can also sense how weak her body feels. She knows that whatever has happened she is now at his mercy.

As she thinks of a plan to escape, Ezekiel starts to awaken. He rubs his eyes and rises from the floor. Eden quickly closes her eyes and pretends to be asleep. Ezekiel looks in her direction and sees that she is unconscious. Thus, he rises and goes outside. Eden opens her eyes to assess how functional her body is. She even searches for a nearby object that she can use as a weapon.

When she hears the handle on the door click, she closes her eyes and tries to slow her breathing. She can hear the water running in the sink. She forces herself to open one eye to see the slave washing himself. He dries himself, turns and begins walking toward Eden.

He sits by her side and places his hand on her forehead. Eden tries to calm her nerves in an effort to control her breathing. That is when she hears him say, "Please wake up. I did not mean to injure you. You have got to get better. Please GOD heal her head. Forgive me for hurting her." Ezekiel walks away from her bedside and goes back outside.

Eden cautiously opens her eyes and looks toward the door. She does not know what to think about what she heard him say. Her mind questions if she should feel afraid of him. She struggles to sit up so that she can look out of the window. Her arms tremble. As she tries to move her legs, the door opens. Ezekiel stands before her. They stare at one another. Eden's breathing becomes labored at the sight of him.

Ezekiel thanks GOD aloud. Although he expresses his gratefulness, she immediately expresses her fear. He holds his hands up as if to plead with her to calm down. "I will not hurt you," he promises. He strives to keep her calm. Eden tries to make demands in her feeble voice that he take her back home immediately. He knows that she is upset and he continues to try and calm her.

Eden threatens, "When my grandmother finds out what you have done to me, you will be killed." He remains silent while she rages.

Males Are To Remain Invisible...

The door slides open to expose the dark corridor of the storage facility. She steps into the hallway with a flashlight that she took from a cart inside the hospital. Elizabeth proceeds down the corridor cautiously.

She stops in front of a unit and inserts a code which opens the storage door and allows her to enter. As she moves beyond the large crates, she finds her love, Lliam. He quickly folds loose pages from a Bible that he has found apparently hidden inside an open box. They hug.

Elizabeth surprises him with food. "There is no way I would allow my hero to starve," she says.

Males Are To Silently Serve...

With his back to the door and his hands held high, Ezekiel slowly moves toward the kitchen area. "You must be hungry," he assumes. Eden stubbornly provides no response. She maintains her stare of disapproval. "You have been out for quite some time. How about I try to get some food for you?" Eden remains silent.

Ezekiel continues to peacefully negotiate, "I have no idea what food would even be available here. This cabin actually belongs to a friend of mine. You may actually remember him from the hospital, or maybe not."

Ezekiel stares at Eden to try to gain some type of approval from her. Based on the wrinkling of her eyebrows, her frown indicated that she had no intent of granting it.

He receives nothing more than angry silence. "Would you at least tell me your name?" he asks.

After his final attempt to communicate, he turns slightly away from her to begin his search through the cabinetry for sources of food. As he becomes more intimidated by her wrath, he whispers to GOD a prayer of survival.

Males Are To Obey...

Ilya's heels click as she paces the floor. She continues to observe Nealon, Milam and Stone through the two-way digital mirror while they kneel. As predicted, Amblin remarks, "They may be ruthless, but you cannot deny how handsome they all are."

Vayl asks Ilya, "Do you seriously plan to allow these dangerous slaves to freely roam our nearby forests? I mean no disrespect princess, but you of all people know how unpredictable and unreliable these slaves are."

Amblin taps her fingers on the table as she listens to Vayl present her arguments to Ilya. "Why would you dare contemplate such a consideration?" Vayl asks.

Ilya turns from the mirror to face her most trusted friends. "You know that I would never allow any male, especially ones as dangerous as these, to roam unsupervised within or outside our gates. I do not trust these males any more than any of you. However, we need these men to do what they do best. They destroy. Without conscience, without heart and without mercy, these men will destroy anything and anyone."

The women look at one another nervously. Amblin boldly asks Ilya if she is referring to Eden. Ilya responds, "None of you want Eden around anymore than I do."

Amblin responds, "Ilya, we can all agree with you that Eden can be annoying. Among the women, she is the saint who does make all of us look bad in comparison. But, why would any of us want her dead? She has done nothing deserving of death. She is smart, beautiful, charming and kind. She is our sister and your blood."

Ilya pauses long before answering. "No. You two are my blood. Eden is nothing more than a huge pending threat who is showing too much mercy towards the males. Her actions are having impact on the other women."

"Releasing these three into the woods to locate her is far better than Eden influencing everyone in this society. If she is allowed to return, she will question everything that grandmother has set in place to protect us. Before we know it, we will inevitably return to our violent past. Can't you all see the danger in her influence?" They slowly begin to express agreement with a silent nod.

Males Are Not To Have Contact With Children...

The warmth from Lliam's body is as calming as the heartbeats heard through his chest. Elizabeth finds temporary escape in his embrace. The peace of the moment is brought to an abrupt halt when Lliam proposes that Elizabeth must get their son into the protection of Pastor Eli's and his sons, Emil and EJ.

Elizabeth silently sheds a tear that she quickly tries to wipe away before it falls onto Lliam's shirt. She asks Lliam, "Why can't we simply take our child, emphasis on the word 'our' and run as far away from this city as our feet will carry us? Our son deserves freedom!" Elizabeth exclaims. Lliam hugs her tightly in order to calm her.

"You are right. But have you ever thought that maybe GOD brought all of us here on purpose, for a purpose?"

Elizabeth withdraws from Lliam and responds defensively, "What do you mean?" Lliam senses her frustration.

He tries to explain. "We have always trusted GOD and He has never failed us. What if now GOD needs to rely on us to heal this land? What if GOD needs to use our son to accomplish that?"

Elizabeth becomes upset. "Stop talking like that!" she demands. "The best thing for you, for me and especially for our son is to leave this place right now." Elizabeth rises and stomps angrily towards the door. Lliam chases her. He stands before the door to stop her from leaving. He tries to console her because he recognizes her fear. He calmly says, "We must get our child to Pastor Eli."

Males Are Never To Be Trusted...

Ezekiel slams the last cabinet door and exclaims, "There is not a thing for us to eat." Eden continues to stare angrily at him in silence. Ezekiel finds himself becoming more comfortable with her expression of hate.

While denying his own feelings of frustration, he suddenly remembers what he saw during his escape. "Wait! There is a creek nearby. We could probably find fish there." Ezekiel searches Eden's face for a positive change in expression, but only gets more frowning.

Without trying to cause Eden any further upset, Ezekiel selects tools and utensils from a closet. He walks toward the bed and extends an empty bucket to her. "If we work together, we can find food." Eden stubbornly refuses to take the bucket. Ezekiel pleads, "Please?"

Males Should Silently Submit...

Between the heaviness of the humidity and the coverage of the clouds, the walk proved exhausting for Eden. She is still struggling with a slight headache from her previous fall. She finds herself falling further behind.

"Would you like to stop and get water? We are near," Ezekiel asks as he slows his pace. Eden remained silent. "Well, this ought to be interesting. Clearly, you refuse to speak to me. Would it be okay if I speak to you? I simply wanted to know your name," he asks.

Eden continues to follow slightly behind him in silence. "I know that you were raised to HATE males, but if you give me a chance then you may find me to be a very nice male. Okay, you probably hate the very sound of my voice," Ezekiel says in hopes of getting Eden to speak.

"I am not your enemy. Maybe you are probably wishing that I would shut up." Ezekiel waits yet for even a hint of a response from her, but all he hears are her footsteps struggling in the gravel.

Ezekiel stops and looks back at Eden. He can see that she is sweating and limping. He approaches her and asks, "Are you hurt?" With the predictable unresponsive silence from Eden, Ezekiel kneels down to examine her foot. Eden pulls away. Ezekiel reminds her that he is the only one around who can help her. Thus, she surrenders to him.

Ezekiel removes her shoe to find that she has several blisters. He jokes, "These elaborate shoes don't seem to be meant for travel through the rough terrain of this forest." She frowns. However, she does allow herself to be vulnerable for a moment in order to lean on him. She lets him help her make her way to the water.

Ezekiel suggests, "You can wash up here while I fish further up. If you need me, feel free to yell, or whisper or send up smoke signals. You have my permission to communicate by whatever method you prefer. By the way, my name is 'Ezekiel' just in case you were wondering." Eden purses her lips in frustration as she sits on the bank. She finds his name to be rather archaic. Yet, the phonetics of his name seem to be descriptive of his strong demeanor.

Meeting A Friend ...

Elizabeth departs from where Lliam is hiding near the base of the city gates. She is carrying what appears to be laundry in an effort not to draw attention to herself. She approaches the rear entrance of the palace gates where she searches frantically for a way to enter. It did not take long for her to realize that she had no authorization code.

A female guard approaches and asks, "Is there a problem?" Elizabeth in her nervousness avoids eye contact while providing an answer. Before she can respond, Mr. Shale appears. He picks up her basket of laundry. "Please forgive me for failing to be here on time," he says to Elizabeth. Once the guard observes their interaction, she departs.

Elizabeth nervously follows Mr. Shale into the palace dining hall. She is at a loss for words. She has no idea who he is or where they are going. She continues to follow quietly. They enter a series of hallways until they come to an isolated room. Mr. Shale places the laundry on the table and turns to look at Elizabeth. She avoids his gaze and with a quiver in her voice she thanks him.

Mr. Shale asks, "Who are you?" Elizabeth tries to act offended at his question and attempts to exit the room. Mr. Shale steps in front of the door. "Miss, I may have been born at night, but it wasn't last night. I know that you are not a citizen of this citadel."

Elizabeth begins to tremble. Mr. Shale says, "Unless you intend to bring harm to the queen or her granddaughters, there is no need for you to be afraid. But you may want to tell me who you are and why you are here." Elizabeth insists that she has no intention of harming anyone.

"I need help. I need someone who I can trust. I must save my baby," she insists.

Mr. Shale confirms, "I suspected you were not from here."

Elizabeth becomes anxious. She asks, "Why do you say that?"

Mr. Shale responds. "Your clothing seems questionable. You used the entrance marked for the slaves. Moreover, you are asking me to help you rescue your infant son."

Elizabeth asks, "Why do you think my baby is a male?" He removes a linen handkerchief from his tunic and extends his hand. "If your child were a female, you would have no need for this," he says as he offers her the handkerchief to dry her tears. Mr. Shale tries to calm her. "I am on your side. I wouldn't wish for anyone's son to be enslaved any more than you would. So, I guess you are meeting someone whom you can trust." Elizabeth widens her eyes.

"It would help if you would tell me your name," he asks. As she reveals herself, Mr. Shale cautions, "You will need someone who can help you. You need someone who has influence. You definitely need someone who would care. There is only one problem. That person seems to be missing. Her name is Eden and she is the queen's youngest granddaughter. I am Mr. Shale, her personal servant. She is the only person who would dare help."

Elizabeth responds, "What do you mean she is missing?"

Mr. Shale states, "It was announced that she is away working on a resource project. However, she has been missing since the day some slaves escaped. I suspect that she has been kidnapped."

Elizabeth tries to swallow in guilt as she recalls the memory of Lliam and Ezekiel trying to carry the unconscious woman out of the city gate. Elizabeth asks, "She is a princess?"

Mr. Shale replies, "Eden is the most kind of the royals. She is not next in line to rule. Her cousin, Ilya, is. She would be the least kind of all the royals. Those two couldn't be more opposite in personality and morality. Princess Ilya would never help you save your son," he warns. "If you want your son back, we must find Eden." Elizabeth remains quiet in her guilt.

Uninvited Struggle...

Ezekiel finds frustration in trying to catch fish with his bare hands while standing waist-deep in the powerful rush of the water. The tasks consume him so much that he is unaware of Eden's struggles downstream.

Eden examines the terrain to see if an escape from Ezekiel is even a possibility. Before she can consider escape she must relieve the pain from her foot. She searches for a strong branch that she can use to balance her weight while she tries to clean herself near the water. She clings to the branch while reaching into the water with the other hand. The branch snaps. She falls in. Eden's scream gets muffled by the water. She fights the currents until she is able to grasp some vines along the bank. She pulls herself to the shore. The weight of her dress makes her climb out of the water more exhausting.

Eden falls to the ground gasping for breath. She opens her eyes and rubs them. Her vision is still blurred. She attempts to stand to her feet when she feels a strong grip around her arm. Before she can scream, another hand gets secured over her mouth. Eden's eyes grow wide with fear. She immediately recognizes the scar on the arm of the hand covering her mouth. Eden fights to be free as soon as she realizes that her attackers are slaves.

Eden bites the hand covering her mouth. His hand begins to bleed. Her scream is silenced when she is struck by one of her three attackers.

Required Dress...

He hands her articles of clothing and shoes. "You seem to be her size," Mr. Shale presumes as he hands Elizabeth the elaborate garments. Elizabeth can't help but to caress the elegant fabrics in her hands. The beautiful clothes that Mr. Shale provided feel like silk and possess a fragrant divine smell of lavender.

Mr. Shale grants her privacy by looking out the window. While she undresses, she asks, "Are you really a slave here? You speak about Eden as if she were family?" Mr. Shale smiles and answers, "I have known Eden and her family since before the war. She is my family. She makes me proud. It has never been a burden to serve her, because I have loved watching her grow."

Elizabeth says, "You love her yet she treats you as a slave?"

Elizabeth emerges dressed in the finest bronze dress that would deem her worthy of standing in this society. Mr. Shale smiles in approval and says, "Eden has never treated me as a slave. Even the queen would never treat me in such a manner. They are aware that I not only know their hearts. I know their secrets."

Elizabeth spins around in an effort to model her new attire. "You could now pass for a royal," Mr. Shale says.

Elizabeth reaches for his hand and says, "I know that you miss her." Elizabeth lowers her head in shame briefly before she lifts it again. She states, "You have been so kind. I promise that she will be returned safely." Mr. Shale appears confused.

Elizabeth can tell by the expression on his face that she has only increased his concern. She continues, "This is so difficult to explain. But, I think that I have already met the woman that you faithfully serve." Elizabeth lets go of Mr. Shale's hand and walks toward the window. "I think that the woman of whom you have been speaking was the same woman who helped me in the hospital a couple of days ago. This woman was quiet, but regal. She possessed authority, but it was evident that she showed concern for me and for my son."

"Where is she?" he asks. Elizabeth turns towards him. "I don't know exactly, but maybe we can find her and rescue my son. We can do it together," she pleads.

As he agrees, Elizabeth says, "Now that I have met you, I can see how she grew to have such a caring spirit."

Mr. Shale responds, "I wish that I could take such credit. But, there is a man, an honorable man, who legitimately could. He may also be able to help you get your son."

A Welcomed Hero...

Ezekiel is startled by the high pitched scream. He drops the fish he caught and immediately follows the sound along the river. As he moves through the trees, the sound of scuffling grows louder. Through the leaves and brush, he sees three men assaulting Eden. At the sight, he recalls his mother's memory and instantly becomes enraged.

With a make-shift cane, he strikes one of the men from behind. Immediately, he turns to confront the second attacker who appeared more muscular than himself. Ezekiel quickly locates vines which are hanging within his immediate reach and wraps them around the neck of the second attacker. Thus, Ezekiel is able to force the man's body into the river. Then, Ezekiel combats the third man with his bare hands. He delivers one fistful blow after another until he renders the third attacker unconscious.

Winded and bloodied, Ezekiel staggers around to find Eden lying unconscious. He examines her to see if she is breathing. Her pulse is weak. He gathers all of his remaining strength and carefully picks up her body. Every step he takes is labored. Nevertheless, he does not waiver in his efforts to get her to the safety of the dwelling where they were hiding.

Once inside the distressed-wooden cabin, he gently places Eden's body onto the bed. He removes her wet clothes and wraps her in a blanket.

His eyes are irritated from the trickling of blood and sweat. He walks to the sink to rinse his face. His hands tremble. He closes his eyes to allow the coolness of the air to calm him. Night is coming. He gathers kindling wood and a flint stone in order to start a fire in the hearth. As the flames rise, the heat starts to fill the room. He is so overwhelmed that he is unaware of his tears. Through the blurriness of his tears, he sees a stack of books on the floor next to the desk. Ezekiel scans the titles of every book until he sees one marked HOLY BIBLE.

He reaches for it and removes some of the dust. The pages were darkened and stuck together. He opens to John 16 verse 33 and reads, "I have told you these things, so that in me you may have peace. In this world you will have trouble. But take heart I have overcome the world..." He begs, "Please help me GOD," and falls asleep.

Males Are To Shield...

Eden holds the baby tight against her chest. She watches Ezekiel battle the male attackers. Eden begins to run. With each footstep, she feels that she can hardly move. She looks behind her and sees no one. The baby is crying. She stops to uncover the baby. That is when she realizes the baby is a male. Yet, despite his gender, his face is so endearing.

As the sky becomes overcast, she examines her surroundings. She is startled at a woman standing motionless before her. Eden tries to speak, but is unable. Eden can hardly make out her face.

The woman begins to speak. "He is not your enemy. Do not forsake him." The woman immediately disappears, when Eden sees the man with the scar reaching out to choke her.

The dream is interrupted when Eden coughs. She holds her neck while struggling to open her eyes. Her body feels cold. She reaches for the blanket and discovers that she is naked. Immediately, she sits up and covers herself in panic. That's when she sees Ezekiel lying on the cold floor. He appears to be asleep and shivering.

Eden struggles to remember what happened. She is almost afraid to examine her own body because she fears she may find signs that she may have been violated while she was unconscious. She carefully opens the blanket and looks at herself. Bruises are visible on her wrist and arm. Her neck feels tender. That is when she remembers the men attacking her.

She searches the room for her clothing. Her frustration grows when she sees them hanging by the fire. She quietly manages to get dressed and not wake Ezekiel. Then, she moves towards the door in an effort to escape. She recalls the woman in her dream reminding her not to "forsake" him. The thought disturbs her.

Eden slowly turns around to look at Ezekiel. His shivering has worsened. She lets go of the handle on the door and walks towards him. When Eden bends down to touch his forehead, she sees his wounds. His forehead feels hot and wet. She immediately alarmed. tries to move his body to the bed. It is a struggle because of his size. She then covers him with the blanket to warm him.

Males Are Discouraged From Friendships...

Bypassing the heavy security at the hospital proved to be easy with Mr. Shale posing as a servant for Elizabeth. They arrive at the male infant ward. Elizabeth searches for her baby through the glass. Mr. Shale recognizes her maternal look. Elizabeth attempts to withhold tears. Mr. Shale says, "If we are going to save him, then we cannot do so staring through this window all day."

Elizabeth agrees and she follows Mr. Shale. They quietly follow a nurse into a restricted clinic area. The steel door slides closed behind them. Elizabeth walks around the room nervously. She asks, "Where are we?" Mr. Shale assures her that hopefully they are in the right place to find the one person who could possibly help them. Suddenly, the steel door begins to slide open. They hide.

They hear the voices of females giving instructions to slaves. Soon, the women depart. Mr. Shale peeks to see who is left inside the clinic. That is when he begins to smile and move towards the center of the room out of her view.

Elizabeth is terrified and remains hidden. She hears something drop to the floor. She is afraid to see what is happening. Before long, she hears the voice of Mr. Shale instructing her to come out. Carefully, she surfaces only to witness Mr. Shale hugging some older gentleman. They are all smiles. "Pastor Eli, meet Elizabeth. This is Pastor Eli, a former king." Elizabeth stares at Pastor Eli's extended hand.

Mr. Shale recognizes her awkwardness and interrupts, "You may want to shake his hand." Elizabeth inhales deeply, apologizes, reaches for his hand and bows. In recognition of his former position as king, Elizabeth pleads, "Your highness, please forgive my ignorance."

Mr. Shale smiles in an effort to comfort Elizabeth. Then, he announces, "Next to Eden, this is the only other person who could help you get your son back." Elizabeth thinks Mr. Shale is making this statement because Pastor Eli held the position of king.

Mr. Shale places his hand on Pastor Eli's shoulder and makes the following confirmation. "Much like Eden, Pastor Eli cares." Mr. Shale pauses to share a moment of silence with Pastor Eli. Elizabeth notices tears in their eyes as Mr. Shale continues, "Or, should I say, Eden would care exactly like her father." Elizabeth can only stare in confusion at this news.

Roles Are Switched...

Before the fire diminishes, Eden puts the remaining wood into the fireplace. She knows that Ezekiel's body requires heat in order to heal.

She searches the cabinets for any medicine to give to Ezekiel. She finds a bottle of expired analgesic and rubbing alcohol. She removes the dust before opening.

However, it proves more difficult to force the pills down his throat because he is unconscious. Nevertheless, she administers rubbing alcohol to his wounds. Slightly he winces, but remains asleep.

She studies him sleeping while the fire crackles loudly. She walks back to the area in front of the fireplace where he was lying. She opens a bag that she noticed he had carried to the river.

Inside, she finds folded pieces of sheet music with photos. The photos contain images of several males and females laughing together which was a foreign concept to Eden. Nevertheless, she finds the photo encouraging.

Before she closes the bag, she discovers a chain with a cross attached. The metal was so polished that its luster seemed to illuminate the room. Eden laid the cross atop the back of her hand and stared at it. She wondered what made this fragile metal object so significant. Within seconds of contemplating that question, she looked down and finds a book.

The stained and worn pages draw Eden. She turns it over to discover it is a Bible. Part of her is afraid to read it because it is censored literature according to the law. Yet, she is curious. She begins reading chapter 4 in the book of Esther.

> "Do not think that because you are in the king's house you alone of all the Jews will escape. For if you remain silent at this time, relief and deliverance for the Jews will arise from another place, but you and your father's family will perish. And who knows but

that you have come to your royal position for such a time as this?"

"Esther replied, 'Go gather together all the Jews who are in Susa and fast for me. Do not eat or drink for three days, night or day... When this is done, I will go to the king, even though it is against the law. And if I perish, I perish..."

At these words, Eden is overwhelmed. Her mind races because at the thought of this woman's actions. "She defied the law to save people?" Eden mumbles her thoughts to herself. She continues, "A woman saves a nation? This is inside the Bible?" This is when Eden begins to question in her mind why the Bible is forbidden literature.

She then turns the pages and finds herself in the book of Matthew. She stumbles onto the story of Joseph and Mary. Fear overwhelms her when she reads about Joseph's decision to marry this woman despite Mary being pregnant because she knows the law her grandmother set forbids marriage. Yet, she in intrigued.

She is reminded of the brutality of males who attacked by the river. But then, her thoughts become conflicted as she recalls the lifetime kindness that Mr. Shale has shown her. Plus, she has received tremendous protection and care from Ezekiel. In that moment, a heavy sense of doubt overcomes her mind. As she recalls the slave suffocating her with his hand earlier that day, she seriously considers the defensive wounds covering Ezekiel's hands and arms.

"Why would he save me?" she questions herself sympathetically while she watches him sleep.

Tracking The Slaves...

Vayl enters Ilya's quarters. "I hope you are bringing good news to my morning," Ilya says as she dresses herself in ornate royal attire. Vayl informs Ilya that the slaves have been tracked to the northeast corner of the forest by the river. "It appears as though they have been sleeping there all night," Vayl says.

Ilya asks, "Can we get visual on them?" Vayl reports that the winds have caused system interference.

The door monitor sounds announce the arrival of Amblin. She rushes inside to inform Ilya that her grandmother is concerned about the whereabouts of Eden. Ilya panics. She issues a command to Vayl, "Find those slaves."

Unusual Bonding...

Ezekiel's sleep is interrupted by his severe coughing. Eden quickly responds by giving him water. He swallows in an effort to gather energy to speak. "You stayed?" he says surprisingly. "In case you were unaware. You are free to go," he teases. His coughing continues. Eden offers no response. "Clearly, I am in no condition to make you stay," he says in the midst of his coughing. He insists, "You probably should go while there is plenty of daylight. Take whatever you need for your journey. We are not far from your city." Eden continues to stare at him in silence.

"You do not need to stay and worry about me. Battling your friends in the woods must have taken a toll on me. I will recover soon," he says. Still, Eden says nothing.

Ezekiel continues to engage conversation. "My father used to tell me how hard it was to put a smile on a woman's face. He used to say that if a woman hates you, she can hold a grudge forever. But my father had a gift for making my mother smile, even when she stubbornly tried not to. If he had not been killed, he probably could have saved my mom from those men. The love my parents had for one another made this world more beautiful." Ezekiel sought a response from Eden.

"You had parents that lived together?" she asks.

Ezekiel suppressed his irritation at her response. He found her question to be seemingly naïve and ignorant. He simply answered, "Yes. My parents loved each other tremendously up until the day they died." Nevertheless, as their conversation continued, Ezekiel began to realize that much of what he was saying sincerely intrigued Eden. With each question she asked, more humility followed.

"How did they die?" Eden asked.

"My father was a pilot and a very loving father. He was killed in a crash. He was brave man and treated others with respect and care. He was a GOD-fearing man. I think if he had had a daughter instead of me, he would have been a force to be reckoned with because he was so protective of my mother. I think that is why I was always so protective of my mother. He died when I was 15. My mother used to tell me that I acted just like him," he coughed.

"She would sing to me all the time. She taught me how to play the piano," Ezekiel said.

"What happened to her?" Eden asked.

Ezekiel seemingly hesitated in responding. "One morning some men came to our home. They brutalized my mom. I did not exactly witness what happened to her because they had me trapped inside of our storage. But I could hear her fighting. I know she fought to protect me. I also know that I will never forget that scar because it was the only mark that I could clearly see through the small opening in the doorframe," Ezekiel says.

Eden immediately recalls the scar on the wrist of the slave who covered her mouth.

Male Contemplation...

Sweat falls from his brow as he pushes his body to its limits. Lliam is trying to maintain his sanity through exercise. There is tremendous exertion with each push-up. Exhaustion finally mandates he rest. As he recovers, Lliam worries how he will save his family. Lliam becomes overwhelmed with thoughts of despair and defeat. He begins to feel that he has failed to protect Elizabeth and their son. He cries out, "GOD, what do you want from me? I don't know what to do. How do I save them? Please help us GOD! Please save my son! Please do not give up on us!"

Lliam wipes the tears from his eyes and with his head lowered he sees the cords along the baseboards. He stands up and follows them amidst the items stacked in the massive storage room where he is hiding. He discovers a computer terminal. There is a monitor nearby. He removes the tarps that are covering boxes, bins and equipment and carefully inspects the array of gadgets that he has found.

The first bin that he opens contains several catalogues and instruction manuals. He opens another bin which contains discs, videos and reels of films. Another box contains newspapers wrapped in plastic bags. Lliam sits on the floor and begins to read.

He reads aloud. "Date is January 16, 2027." Lliam continues to scan the titles before he reads a sentence that interests him. Again, he reads aloud, "King Eli sanctions the debridement facilities for homeless orphans five months prior to elections." Lliam tries to adjust his vision to see better. The caption line under the photo identifies one of the men as King Eli. Liam rubs his forehead because the man in the photo looks like a younger version of Pastor Eli.

Nursing The Patient...

Eden wipes the sweat from Ezekiel's forehead. With the back of her hand she checks him for fever as he sleeps. She watches his chest rise and fall recalling the words, "This man is not your enemy." Her thoughts are interrupted by a cold draft. She notices that the fire is dying. Before she moves toward the fire place, she covers Ezekiel with a heavy blanket.

Eden places kindling in the fireplace to intensify the heat. She sits on the hearth and stares intently at the flames. The heat comforts her and she begins to feel weary. Her eyes search the room for another blanket to cover herself. Yet, she has no desire to move away from the fire.

The flames illuminate the pages of the Bible which catches her attention. She picks it up and turns the pages. Her eyes settle on first on 1 Corinthians 11 and begins to read aloud to herself, "In the Lord, however, woman is not independent of man, nor is man independent of woman. For as a woman came from a man, so also man is born of woman. But everything comes from GOD." Eden quickly closes the Bible in nervousness at the discovery of this passage. She found the words frightening because they contradict the fundamentals she had been taught regarding males.

Nevertheless, just like a child who had been restricted from touching or handling something as dangerous as fire, Eden desired to know more. Once again, she opens and begins browsing the pages of the Bible. Her eyes were becoming extremely heavy. Thus, she made herself read aloud to fight against falling asleep. "1 John 3...This is how we know we are the children of GOD."

Another female voice continues, "...anyone who does not do what is right is not God's child. 1 John 5...This is how we know we love the children of GOD: by loving GOD and carrying out His commands." Eden anxiously searches for the voice. "Whomever does not love their brother or their sister whom they have seen, cannot love GOD whom they have not seen..." the voice states.

Her voice quivering, Eden asks, "Are you the GOD?"

"I am not GOD," the voice says. Eden rubs her eyes in an attempt to remove the blurriness from her vision. That is when she notices the long locks of blonde hair. Eden is able to focus on the bright image of the woman standing before her. "It is time for you to know GOD. ONLY He can help you save the child."

Eden asks, "What child?"

The woman places her hand over Eden's hand and says, "You must learn trust to in GOD more than in yourself." Next, bright beams of light blind Eden. She shouts, "Wait!" Suddenly, Eden awakens to the flash of lightning coming through the window. The sound of strong winds howling outside alarms her. She rubs her eyes to clear her vision. She searches the room. Ezekiel is missing.

The Queen Falls...

Ilya enters her grandmother's quarters. Many attendants surround the queen. Ilya is overwhelmed at the sight of her unconscious grandmother. "Princess Ilya," a voice says. It is the queen's physician. She approaches Ilya with an embrace. Ilya inquires, "What happened?"

The doctor reveals, "The queen sustained a head injury from a fall. Apparently, she has been neglecting herself by not eating or sleeping. She fell and hit her head. Her vitals did show dehydration and discrepancies in her blood and hormone levels." Ilya could hardly breathe.

The doctor continued, "It was brought to my attention that her stress may have been due to the fact that Eden is away." Ilya had little response. "We can monitor her condition and reduce the swelling in her head. But, it may help to find Eden and alert her to what is happening. Who knows? Maybe, the mere sound of Eden's voice may help your grandmother start to heal more quickly." Ilya nodded in agreement.

Ilya approached the queen's bedside. She grasped her hand. "I am here for you grandmother. I know that you can hear me. I promise to take care of everything. Do not worry." Her tears fall onto the queen's hand. When she leans onto the bed, she feels the unusual bulkiness of an object. Ilya slips her hand between the mattresses and pulls out what appears to be a journal.

Purposely Hidden...

The cold hard surface of the floor served as a sufficient bed for Lliam. He slept with a small box for a pillow and a tarp as his blanket. Lliam rested soundly until the break of the seal of the storage door slid open. He was startled by footsteps. He slid his body behind some large boxes and tried to remain extremely still.

"Lliam, where are you?" a female voice whispered.

Lliam recognized that voice. He peeked his head around the corner. It was her. The room was dimly lit. From his view he was able to make out three figures which caused him to retreat more into his hiding place.

"Lliam, it's Lizzie. Please come out. It's okay."

Lliam slowly arises from his hiding place. Elizabeth locates him in the darkness and runs to him. She embraces him. "Please come and meet these men," she says. As she guides him out, Lliam is able to adjust his eyesight enough to recognize one of the men from the male containment unit.

"I see that you made it out my friend," says Pastor Eli. They embrace. Lliam is elated. "What are you doing here?" Lliam asks. Elizabeth explains how she met Mr. Shale and how he introduced her to Pastor Eli. She also explains how Pastor Eli can help them get their son back. "But first we must locate Eden," she says. Lliam is confused because he has no idea who Eden is.

Assuming Complete Leadership...

Heavily surrounded by her security team, Ilya enters the formal council hall. The chatter in the room fades as the council members watch Ilya walk toward the chair reserved for the queen. Everyone sits before Vayl speaks.

"Thank you for gathering under such a short notice. This meeting was called with urgency in light of the queen's medical condition. We are all aware of the head trauma that our queen endured. Currently, she is resting comfortably and is receiving the best medical care. We have no doubt that she will make a full recovery," Vayl reassures.

"In the meantime, I assure everyone that we are not without competent leadership. Our queen has trained her successor to govern us with courage, intelligence, passion and ambition. Princess Ilya will step into the role of leadership in the absence of our queen as long as this nomination is not met with any objections," Vayl bids.

One member of the council voices her concern. "With regard to the queen's health, we need to consider one factor. The queen was extremely concerned about the whereabouts of Eden. We are equally concerned. Clearly, we know that Eden did serve in the capacity of raising awareness regarding issues of justice and morality. In fact, her perspective proved invaluable to all of us. The queen always considered Eden's opinions for a reason and right now Eden's perspective seems most needed. I would think that Princess Ilya would rule best with Princess Eden by her side."

Mumbling among the members follows. Amblin rises to address the council. She states, "Thank you so much governess. You are completely correct that locating Eden is of the utmost importance. Her absence combined with the queen's condition has made this an extremely difficult time for us all. However, if anyone could lead during this time, Princess Ilya can. She was raised under the same guidance as Eden and embodies that same wisdom. She was not only trained for this moment. She was born for this moment."

Amblin continues, "She has the passion it requires to advance and protect our world so that our enemies cannot harm us in the midst of confusion. She will make us an even more powerful force in the future. We can trust her with our lives. Moreover, we can trust her with our daughters' lives." Council members slowly begin to nod in agreement.

Unexpected Confession...

She pushes the heavy wooden door open against the wind and steps onto the dilapidated porch. She watches Ezekiel from a distance as he is bowed down and on his knees. Eden approaches him. The blowing of the wind slightly mutes the sound of his voice even though he is speaking aloud. His eyes are closed. She watches and listens. Ezekiel is praying.

"GOD what have we done? How do we fix this? GOD, please forgive the men and the women. Please remove the pain from the hearts of the women. Please help me to forgive the men who killed my mother," he cries.

Even though the sounds of the winds are increasing, Ezekiel can hear the distinct crunch of leaves and the snap of loose twigs. He speculates that Eden may be approaching. He wipes his tears and gathers himself. He senses Eden nearing.

Ezekiel remains on his knees but he allows the gusts to lift his head. He says, "I released you. You are free to return to your city. Why have you remained here?" With a long pause, he looks back to view her. Her hair partially hides her face. She is locked into her familiar stance of stubborn silence. Ezekiel in frustration bows.

Without saying a word, Eden starts to walk away. Her steps are interrupted with four words. "I lied to you," he says. Suddenly, she stops in order to figure out if the sounds of the winds distorted his words. She holds her breath at the anticipation of what he will say next.

Ezekiel rises from his knees. "I know the men who attacked you." The sadness that Eden was feeling for him begins to transform into upset and doubt. She turns to face him.

Ezekiel begins. "I remembered exactly who they were when your soldiers first captured all of us. The man with the scar is Nealon. I would recognize that that scar anywhere. That scar belongs to the man who killed my mother." Eden is speechless.

She walks toward him as he continues, "I never thought that I would ever see those men again until that day when I found myself shackled alongside the man with the scar. While all the other men were thinking of how to free themselves, I was actually thanking GOD for reuniting me with my mother's murderer. Maybe GOD was finally giving me approval to avenge my mother's death."

Eden had not realized that she was frowning in response to his words. "When I saw him harming you by the river, all those memories of my mother's attack came flooding back. I had to save you. I refused to let him kill again."

Eden dropped to her knees in front of Ezekiel and bowed her head in disbelief. Ezekiel sat on an adjacent tree stump. He explained, "It was my fault in the first place that he even had access to harm you. I dragged you all the way out here when I should have left you in that hospital. You needed treatment but I was not thinking. I did not want to bring you with me. We panicked. I panicked. I was trying to help a friend save his son."

"You are speaking of the woman with the infant in the male containment unit at the hospital?" Eden asked. "They are your friends?"

Ezekiel nodded. Eden sighed. It was difficult for her to believe this man cared enough to sacrifice his safety for his friends. It was contrary to what she has been taught about the male species. "I do not understand. The woman is also your friend? How can a woman be friends with a male slave?" she asks.

"Why does this surprise you? Men and women can be just friends. Although, there is a reality that every person we see is basically the result of a man and a woman becoming "friends". If your parents had not been friends, to put it mildly, you would not exist," he says.

Eden explains that where she comes from, males are an unpredictable and cruel enemy. Their friendship is not required to produce offspring which explains the need for the male breeding unit. "Only select males are housed in the breeding unit. These males must be of stellar quality in intelligence, strength and non-violent behavior."

"Something tells me that you have never had a friend who is a male," he speculates. Yet, Eden's reaction to his comment is silently subdued. "Do you have a father or perhaps a brother in your life?" he asks.

Eden was surprised that she did not feel offended at his inquiry. She wrestles to provide an answer because she feels a hint of shame at the only answer that she feels compelled to share. "They are to serve only as slaves. Grandmother has instilled that in me for years which is why she kept me shielded the influence of the males," she explains as she lowers her head.

The awkward silence that followed was broken by his response. "I can see that your grandmother served as your source of guidance, affection and protection. Clearly, she filled a dual parental role and instilled in you what she thought was best," Ezekiel says before he asserts. "But, only a father can instill true self-worth." At these words, her mind recalls only one male who fit this descriptive role of validation in her life. That would be Mr. Shale.

Restructuring Begins...

Outside the palace, the gathering crowd can be heard. Ilya peers through the panes in the balcony doors. Amblin approaches from behind and says, "Everyone is awaiting your arrival." Ilya puts her head down. "What's the matter? This the moment we have dreamed of." Amblin shakes Ilya's shoulders in order to place a smile on her face. "You are to become our new leader and rule even better than your grandmother. This is no time to become timid."

Ilya looks back out of the window at the crowd below. She whispers, "You promise to stay by my side, Amblin?"

Vayl approaches with news. "Pardon me princess but the prisoners have been placed in solitary quarters away from the general population as you instructed." Ilya is relieved. "Okay, good. We never want them to reveal what we have done."

They are interrupted by a council representative. "The governor is ready to announce Princess Ilya as the new leader." Ilya and Amblin lock eyes. Amblin says, "Are you ready to make us proud?"

Males Are Not To Engage...

Seated silently they allow the strength of the wind to calm them. Ezekiel asks, "How old are you?" Eden tilts her head to the side in an effort to decide if she wants to provide him with an answer. "Why?" she asks.

Ezekiel senses that she is irritated. Before he can answer, hard pellets of cold rain drops rapidly began to pound their bodies and the ground around them. They make a run for the door.

Ezekiel slams the door shut. They both are breathing hard. Eden positions herself directly in front of the fire place so she can capture the heat. Ezekiel says, "If you don't want to become ill, then you may want to get out of those wet clothes."

Eden opposes his suggestion. "I will be okay," she said.

"Forgive me. I was not trying to be disrespectful." Then, Ezekiel asks, "Do you mind if I remove my wet clothes?" Eden awkwardly allows it.

Ezekiel removes his tunic. Eden turns away to show respect. Ezekiel laughs. Eden asks why he is laughing. Ezekiel responds, "I distinctly remember where I first saw you. It was your dark colored eyes staring at me. You were at the lab standing over me. I guess I now find it humorous that you look away."

In that instant, Eden looks down at her wrist and remembers that he was the captive who gripped her while he laid on the table. She remembered his eyes.

Not Alone...

"It is getting dark outside," Mr. Shale responds. As Elizabeth and Lliam embrace, Pastor Eli reassures them that he will help them get their son back safely.

Lliam proposes, "Pastor Eli, we trust you. If we don't make it, will you please take care of our son?"

Pastor Eli states, "There is no need for talk like that, Lliam. You will live because your son will need you. He will need you to teach him GOD's truth. He will need you to protect and train him. Besides, I do not believe the deliverance of your child will be at the hand of any of us in this room." They all stare at Pastor Eli in confusion.

Pastor Eli continues. "There is a woman who was born and rightfully trained for such a time as this. Even though I failed her, GOD did not. It will be by her bravery, her wisdom and especially by her willful sacrifice that your son will not only be saved. Your son will lead." Lliam wonders of whom he is speaking and how does he know these things.

Pastor Eli says, "I know I sound like an irrational old fool. But please believe me when I say that your son is special. He will restore unity, hope and healing to every heart here. Hope always comes when someone loves enough to lay down their life even for their enemy."

Males Are Not To Question...

The steel door slides open. Vayl and her soldiers enter the sterile quarantined quarters on the enslavement unit. "Rise!" the guard orders. Nealon, Stone and Milam stand and immediately drop to their knees at the sight of Princess Ilya. Amblin is by her side.

"You are all aware that I possess the power to release you from your bond to our kingdom?" Ilya asks. None of the men dare make eye contact for it is forbidden.

"I understand that you failed in your task. Apparently, she is still alive." The slaves offered no response. "You all must remain quarantined here. If she returns, she may recognize you as her attackers. That would jeopardize everything. Besides, you reported that in your efforts to eliminate Eden, you were all overcome by another male slave? Is that true?" Ilya inquires.

Nealon requests permission to speak. "A male did come to her rescue. We assumed that he was a slave due to his letter marking B." This news upsets Ilya.

"Is something wrong princess?" Amblin asks. Ilya directs Amblin and Vayl away from the hearing range of the slaves. "Grandmother set up the male breeding unit when we were teens. This was enacted way after the other male slave units were defined. Grandmother and the council realized that they did not want to deny the younger women the opportunity to give birth someday." Amblin questions, "Do you think that Eden ran away knowingly with a slave to have a child? That does not sound like something Eden would do. That sounds like something one of the younger women would do. Eden is too old to dare consider that."

Ilya returns her attention to Nealon. She asks, "What do you know of this male slave?"

Nealon answers, "The male was captured along with us. He spent much of his time with slaves named Eli and Lliam. It is rumored that they are preparing for the coming of a special male child who is to be a deliverer."

This news alarms Ilya. She remains silent. Amblin asks, "Do you think it is possible that a male child is to be born between this slave and Eden?" Ilya inhales deeply. "As far as I am concerned, that will never happen."

Then Amblin suggests, "Maybe we could place these slaves in the same unit with the slave, Eli, so that they could extract more info." Ilya responds, "Maybe I will meet with this slave, Eli, myself."

Sincere Bonding Moment...

Ezekiel joins Eden in front of the fire place. "I think that I collected enough nuts from the trees to hold us over until the storm departs," he says. Eden tries to conceal her happiness at the sight of the nuts because she does not want him to know how famished she is. She grabs a few shells and begins to pry them open. Despite the mess, she places the nuts in her mouth and chews. As she closes her eyes to enjoy the taste, a slight smile comes over her face. She opens her eyes to find Ezekiel staring at her. In embarrassment, she wipes her mouth and thanks him. "You are welcome," he says.

They sit in silence for quite some time and listen to the crackle of the wood. Ezekiel clears his throat, "Would you want to ever marry?" Eden can hardly breathe at the sound of this question.

Ezekiel can sense her anxiety. He apologizes, "I did not mean to upset you. I just thought that a woman like you would make a tremendous wife someday." Still in shock, it takes her a moment to remember to swallow.

Ezekiel offers, "Why don't you get some rest? When morning comes, I can guide you back to your home. There is nothing to hold you here. Besides, you were never my prisoner. I am truly sorry that I took you from your home. I am even more sorry that I put your life in danger. I promise to return you home safely." Ezekiel arises to retrieve a blanket from the bed. He returns to the area in front of the fire place and wraps the blanket around Eden. He says, "Sleep in peace."

As he turns to walk away, Eden speaks up, "Much older, yes and my name is Eden". Ezekiel turns around to face her. "You asked earlier how old I am. I am far older than you. I just happen to have uniquely youthful genes. I have no children. And yes I have imagined marriage. But it violates all the sacrifices of my grandmother, my mother and my cousin. I owe them loyalty. It is because of them that I survived the war. They have taught me everything that I know. Moreover, they protected me from the violence of the males. My entire life after the war has been spent living in a grand palace and being trained to serve my cousin once she becomes the next queen. She is stronger. Grandmother and mother knew that Ilya would become a powerful leader one day. They always told me that I was the sound, wise and humble one who could best counsel my cousin. But, between me, you and your GOD, I wish that were true."

Eden sighs. "No matter how much love and respect I have tried to show my cousin, I strongly sense her hatred. I have never spoken of it because it sounds paranoid. I was not the one other girls wanted to hang around. I was always awkward in conversation. Ilya however could persuade anyone of anything including the slaves. Ilya could enter any room and capture attention. Women listen to her. I on the other hand enter a room only to observe."

"Why do you say that? Are you jealous of her?" he asks.

"Never, I am proud of my cousin. I love her. She has a strength and a determination that I could only dream of possessing. Dare I mention how strikingly beautiful in appearance she is with all of that red hair. She is aware of it. That often confused me about her," Eden says.

Ezekiel interrupts, "The woman on the platform with the fiery red hair is the cousin you speak of?"

She redirects, "Grandmother taught us that we no longer had to utilize our looks to manipulate males or compete with our fellow sisters. We are free from that type of mental bondage in our new order. I guess Ilya felt differently. She enjoyed using her looks and power over the male slaves. She has even falsely accused a few of them of various sight crimes. When in actuality, they were innocent."

Ezekiel asked, "What is a sight crime?"

Eden explained, "Our laws are very strict. They dictate that males are never to look upon our bodies for any reason. But for the sake of sheer sport, Ilya would entrap them in questionable situations."

Ezekiel's eyes widened as Eden spoke. "She would accuse slaves of making eye contact or touching her inappropriately when they were innocently serving her.

All God's *step*-Children

When she would pass by them, she would flip her hair in their faces. If any slave showed the slightest reaction, she emphatically accused them of lust."

Ezekiel was quiet. Eden continued, "I tried to reason with her. Thus, she would insist that the males were uncontrollable animals we had to tame. I told her that maybe it would be in her best interest to stop provoking the uncontrollable animals before she got bit."

Ezekiel smiles and questions, "Animals? Seriously?"

Eden suddenly feels convicted and confesses. "I owe you an apology. We all do. We had no right to enslave you because you are males. We justified our actions based on fears from the past."

After a long awkward pause, Ezekiel shocks Eden with the following statement. "Maybe your grandmother was not completely wrong in enslaving the men," he says as Eden tries to absorb his comment.

Ezekiel continues. "When men ruled, there was no end in sight to their wickedness. Men seemed to allow more and more evil to possess them all because of their desire to please themselves more than GOD. For countless generations men who took innocent people from their homes. It was men who stripped people of any identity. It was men who dehumanized. It was men who stole feelings, decisions and dreams. It was men who created the institution of true slavery."

Eden's eyes fill with tears. Ezekiel sits on the hearth adjacent to her. He says, "It was that type of man who killed my mother. Your grandmother didn't reestablish slavery. It seems as though she was trying to create a barrier to protect all of you and preserve your lives. For that, she could not have been entirely wrong." Eden is at a loss for words.

"Besides, she was creative enough to give you a very powerful name that I happen to like. Thank you for finally telling me what it is," he says.

Darkness Hides Light...

The steel door slides open. Pastor Eli opens his eyes but the dimness makes it difficult to see. Light from the hall illuminates the figures standing before him. He recognizes the female voice. "I understand that it is very late but we have much to discuss, Mr. Eli," she says. Ilya, Vayl and Amblin enter the slave quarters of Pastor Eli while the guards remain in the hallway.

Ilya states, "I remember you from my childhood, Mr. Eli. You have never been a stranger to my family, have you?"

Pastor Eli sits up and rubs his eyes to gather himself. "I have known you your entire life, Princess Ilya and I am not your enemy."

Ilya takes steps closer to the old man. "You have been a mysterious yet constant presence in our lives. I never understood why my grandmother would even allow you to remain alive. You have been around well before I was ever born. Yet, as I became older I had to wonder what significant tie did you have to my family. Well, I found my answer in my grandmother's journal. You are Eden's father, aren't you?" she insists. He is silent.

Time To Return...

Tapping on the door awakens Eden. She looks around the dimly lit room. She observes Ezekiel sleeping. The tapping continues to startle her. She uncovers herself and finds courage to walk over and open the door.

There she finds the baby wrapped in an expensive royal blanket. She uncovers the baby to discover it is male. She examines him. Her compassion is stirred. As she turns to take the baby inside, the front door slams shut. She is grabbed from behind and made to kneel. In terror, she tries to catch her breath. A figure slowly approaches. She squints to see through the darkness. It is Ilya. She takes the baby from Eden's arms. Eden is confused. Ilya departs with the baby while leaving Eden surrounded with the male slaves led by Nealon.

As they prepare to execute her, she looks up to the sky for help. A familiar female voice whispers in her ear. It is the angel. "Do not fear. GOD will strengthen you." Immediately, Ezekiel comes to her rescue and strikes Nealon. Eden awakens from this dream disturbed.

She looks around the room and finds Ezekiel still sleeping soundly. She rises to clean her face and calm herself. She then searches for a writing utensil.

On a worn piece of paper, Eden poetically writes, "You are a slave to no man or woman. You are free. Please forgive us. Please forgive me."

She longingly watches him sleep for a while before she decides where to place this paper. She opens the Bible to Exodus 3. She places the paper on top of this page. She then positions the Bible next to his head. As she kneels beside him and watches him breathe, she wipes the tears from her eyes. She rises to depart.

Dare To Save...

"We cannot free all of the male slaves," Elizabeth warns. "As much as I hate to say it, some of these males are dangerous criminals who need to remain locked up."

Lliam nods in agreement. "Some of the women may be too, but that is another issue."

"If we can reach the queen, then maybe we can convince her to give our son back. We have to show her that we are not the enemy. We don't belong to this world," Elizabeth says.

Lliam confirms, "We must find this woman named Eden. Pastor Eli has already told us how vital she is to the queen. In the meantime, we will rely on the help that GOD has provided with Pastor Eli and Mr. Shale. This brings me to the next proposal. I need to return to the male enslavement units." Elizabeth shakes her head in disagreement. "Are you crazy?" she asks.

"I understand this frightens you, but I need the help of more proficient engineers if I am to access their system. Pastor Eli has two sons who can help us," Lliam says.

"Gaining access to their coding system will allow you access into secure areas, including the palace. Mr. Shale has already given me a badge of a deceased former council member to use to bypass security. I now need to mark this as your identification code," Lliam says.

Ezekiel Awakens...

Ezekiel awakens and finds that the fire has diminished. It is morning. He rubs his eyes to better search the room for Eden. With his head lowered, he gathers himself. That is when he finds the letter.

"I have heard the cries of my people," he reads from Exodus. Her note is found. It does not take long for him to realize that she has returned to her kingdom. His reaction is subdued at first as he begins to pray. Then, a panic sets in, which prompts him to go find her.

Un-welcome Home...

The intensity of the morning heat dehydrates Eden. Nevertheless, she sighs in relief when she sees the gates leading into the citadel. She makes her way to the exterior wall. Her throat is so parched that she can hardly speak in order to alert the guards to her presence. She finds a faucet in the wall and begins to drink. Then, she sits against the wall to rest from her exhaustion. Eden is relieved when she overhears voices. She whispers, "Finally I'm home." She gathers strength to rise so that she can reveal herself to the women of whom she can hear approaching.

Before Eden can speak, she overhears her name. The women are discussing her disappearance. "Sympathizers are equally as dangerous as the slaves themselves. It seems inconceivable that Eden would help males escape. She is the queen's granddaughter," one of them states.

Another woman responds. "Maybe hormones made her desperate for a baby. Eden is older. She could have found it hard to face the queen. We have all struggled with similar thoughts. Still, there is no excuse."

Still hidden, Eden covers her mouth in disbelief. Their accusations leave her speechless and brokenhearted. Once she realizes that she can no longer reveal her return, she must find another way into the city. That is when she recalls the hidden entrance at the water main.

Better Late Than...

"We must get you out of here, father, before the princess has you killed. You know I can get word to Emil," EJ whispers from inside the adjacent cell.

"My son, do not worry. The princess will bring will not harm me. The queen would never allow her," Pastor Eli assures. EJ questions how his father could be so certain.

"The queen values family above everything," Pastor Eli states. EJ is further confused. He starts to assume that senility is making his father's thoughts incoherent. Thus, EJ begs his father to allow him to contact Emile, who helped Liam and Ezekiel escape. "I don't want to involve you or your brother," Pastor Eli says.

"Father, we are your only family. Why are you speaking in such a manner? Are you missing Emile?" EJ asks.

"EJ, I wish that I could have raised you both in the life that a decent father should have. I have failed all of my family in so many ways." Pastor Eli says. EJ can hear his father crying in his cell.

"Father, these cell walls have never prevented you from providing us with the utmost in love, guidance and protection. It was because of you that my brother had the bravery to escape. Please, don't worry. You are our hero," EJ confirms.

"I pray that someday you and your brother will get the rightful opportunity to be free men, fathers and the heroes that I should have been. I want you to be a father who is there for all of your family despite the devastations of life. War does not break a family apart. Cowardice does," Pastor Eli says.

Where It All Started...

Inside hidden tunnels and halls, Eden slips past armed guards to enter the infant male unit at the hospital. She braces herself against the door and closes her eyes to recall details from her dreams. Then, she opens her eyes and observes the babies sleeping.

She places a surgical mask on her face before she proceeds to find the child. It does not take long for her to find the baby from her dream with the distinct birthmark on his foot. She eagerly wraps the blanket around his frame, but the opening of the door interrupts her. She quickly hides among the incubators.

The footsteps approach and stop at this child's station. Eden then hears soft singing. She knows that she has heard that singing before. Thus, she rises to discover it is the woman, Elizabeth, whom she had encountered prior to her kidnapping. Elizabeth locks eyes with Eden once again. They are reunited in their shock and stare.

"You may not believe me, but, I am glad that you have returned safely," Elizabeth says apprehensively.

"You may be correct. Of course, that depends on if you had something to do with my untimely absence or not," Eden says while clearing her throat. A faint muffled sound of the baby can be heard. They both move closer to the baby. Eden cautiously waits for Elizabeth to grant her permission to touch the child by nodding. Eden gently lifts and cradles the child.

Elizabeth watches Eden handle her son. "You should have a child of your own. You would make a good mother." At these words, Eden becomes anxious and places the infant in Elizabeth's arms. Elizabeth hugs the baby tightly.

"You would give up your life for this child?" Eden calmly asks. The tears in Elizabeth's eyes answers Eden's question. Then, Eden asks, "How can you be certain he won't turn out to be a violent and dangerous man?"

Elizabeth forcefully asserts, "Because, I am his mother."

"Well, we had better get your son out of here. We have many minds to change and we must start with the queen." After Eden makes this statement, Elizabeth hesitantly states her doubts about them gaining access to the queen. Yet, Eden assures that they will.

A Way Inside...

"I heard that you need some help breaking and entering," a male voice says from behind. Lliam holds his breath and tries to figure out why the voice sounds so familiar. Lliam musters up enough courage to turn around. He can hardly contain his excitement when he sees Emil's face. They embrace.

"Where have you been? How did you end up here? How did you know that I was here?" Lliam questions.

Emil laughs. "To answer one of your questions, I have been hiding as carefully as you have throughout the citadel since our escape. I actually stumbled upon this abandoned storage facility less than a day ago. That is how I found you.

"It is good to see you," Lliam says with a sigh of relief.

Emil says, "I hid in a container in the next room. I heard male and female voices in conversation. In my lifetime, I have only heard a male voice submit to the demands of a female voice. I had no idea what to think when I overheard the progressive discussion coming from inside this room. Is it true? Is there someone who can truly set free the males?"

"Pastor Eli believes it is so. I too believe. That would mean that I somehow need to reenter the general population of slaves unnoticed," Lliam says.

Emil questions, "Do you think you can get past these armed guards? Keep in mind that these are women. These are the most extremely intelligent women on the earth. You know nothing gets past any woman." Lliam realizes that Emil is correct.

"Well, as my dad, our resident pastor, likes to point out, we will need a miracle from GOD. In the meantime, you have got me. I can get you in." Emil reassures as he places his hand on Lliam's shoulder.

At The Edge...

Ezekiel arrives at the edge of town before day's end. Female guards surround the city gates. He believes that Eden returned to the palace. Thus, he must maneuver past the guards in order to make it to the palace.

Home Sweet Palace...

"How do you know Mr. Shale?" Eden asks Elizabeth. Elizabeth struggles to explain how she met Mr. Shale. However, Eden stops her. "I am not all that surprised that you have encountered Mr. Shale. For a man, he has a way of getting around."

As they quietly enter the palace, Eden suggests they split up. Elizabeth agrees. "Do you think that you can find Mr. Shale?" Eden asks. Elizabeth nods. "You can alert him to what is happening. I trust him more than my cousin. I will find my grandmother," Eden says.

"I thought we were here to find the queen," Elizabeth says. Suddenly, Eden remembers that Elizabeth has no idea that the queen is her grandmother. Eden responds, "Mr. Shale can help us with that. Do not worry. I will find you both soon." They depart from each other.

Water May Be Thicker...

The stately corridors are decorated with portraits of women who have sacrificed their lives to build this new world. Eden finds the hall that leads to her grandmother's quarters. She stands before the portrait of her mother and gently places her fingertips on the image. She wipes her tears and continues to her grandmother's quarters.

A familiar voice startles Eden. "Welcome home, cousin." Eden is frozen in fear. She turns toward the direction of the voice. Ilya is seated adjacent the area of the queen's quarters. "We were all worried about you," Ilya states.

Eden is uncertain what to think because Ilya does not seem too distressed regarding her disappearance. "Where were you?" Ilya asks. Eden is hesitant to answer. As Ilya continues to talk, Eden inquires about their grandmother. Her cousin offers little response. Eden's nervousness is evident.

"You know that even though our mothers were sisters, your mother was grandmother's favorite?" Ilya asks. "It is true you know. Just like you, your mother was modest. She would not allow our grandmother to play favorites between her and her sister, whom she loved very much." Ilya continues. "In fact, our mother's loved and protected one another deeply. Their loyalty was sincere and impressive. Everyone assumes that you and I are exactly like our mothers."

Ilya asks, "This surprises me. I find it difficult to want to love or protect you." Eden remains silent. Ilya shares more. "It just seemed like your mother constantly overshadowed my mother. This in turn meant that you overshadowed me. I did not like that or you very much. I loved your mother, Princess Dianne, tremendously. I am the one who loved and needed her more."

Tears begin to fall from Eden's eyes. "I did cry when your mother passed. But, when you disappeared, I felt relieved. I thought I was finally free of you. Your mere existence always made me feel worthless," Ilya states.

Eden tries to contain her emotions. "Ilya, we are cousins. I love you. I am not your enemy," Eden says. Ilya rises, moves close to Eden and states, "On the contrary, you are very much my enemy. You never got the memo."

A Lineage Divided...

As the slaves from the breeding unit return to their quarters, EJ sees a physician enter his father's cell. In upset, EJ fights to release himself from his shackles. The guards try to contain him, but EJ fights. The guard tries to understand why his behavior suddenly becomes so combative. EJ yells down the hall, "Dad!" The guard orders that he be sedated. A nurse who is called to check his vitals asks, "Why was he sedated?" The guard reports that he resisted.

The nurse looks in the direction of his father's cell. Then, she turns to look at the guard and says, "I realize that he is a slave, but he is also human. And this human is imprisoned here with his father. Did it ever occur to you that maybe he saw the physician enter his father's cell?" The guard offered no response.

The nurse ordered that both Pastor Eli and EJ be taken to the hospital for treatment.

A Cousin Scorned...

Ilya slowly circles around Eden as she continues to voice her disdain. Eden tries to provide an answer. "I have returned because this is my home. I think things can be better and different between our female society and the slaves." Ilya releases a sigh of frustration.

"This is precisely why you must die," Ilya threatens.

Eden cautiously warns Ilya while trying to maintain her own distress at Ilya's statement. "Violence against women is punishable by death and will not be tolerated."

Ilya responds, "So is your treason, cousin. As far as the council is concerned, you are an enemy because you freed a male slave. How dare you, Eden!"

"Grandmother will never allow you to harm me, Ilya." Eden insisted. Yet, before Eden could speak further, guards approached and surround her. "What's happening? Vayl, Amblin, answer me!" Eden asserts.

"Much has changed in the few days that you have been away, Eden. There is new leadership," Ilya says. Eden demands to know the whereabouts of grandmother.

Help Has Arrived...

The lush gardens serves as an ideal hiding place for Ezekiel as he makes his way onto the palace grounds. He has a clear view of the activity inside the palace through the windows.

Several different women traverse the hallway. However, Ezekiel becomes hopeful when he sees Elizabeth darting across. He tries to track her movement down the hallway from the outside. He watches her enter the laundry room. Through the thickness of the glass he notices that Elizabeth has embraced a short-statured aged black male. He is confused at the interaction. In desperation he gently taps on the glass.

Mr. Shale pushes Elizabeth aside to protect her. As the window slides open, Mr. Shale's anxiety grows at the sight of Ezekiel entering. Mr. Shale grabs a broom to defend them. Elizabeth screams, "Wait!" She moves in front of Mr. Shale once she recognizes it is Lliam's friend. She then helps Ezekiel enter the laundry room.

Life Is Short...

Beeps from the heart monitors fill the hospital room. EJ struggles to open his eyes. He gradually turns his head to see his father lying in the bed next to him. His throat is dry and inflamed. Yet, EJ tries to call out to Pastor Eli. "Father, can you hear me." EJ gets no response. EJ tries to sit up and exit his hospital bed.

EJ makes his way to his father's bedside and grasps his hand to pray. "GOD, I know you love and care for my dad. Please have mercy on him and heal him. Please allow him to continue his work to unify the men and women." He places his head on his dad's chest to listen to his heartbeat. He feels his father's warm breaths moving the strands of his hair.

EJ lifts his head to find his father awake. "Aren't you a sight for these old eyes," Pastor Eli whispers. EJ just wipes his tears and smiles. "How do you feel dad?" EJ asks. His father coughs and says he feels alive. They laugh weakly. Pastor Eli requests water. EJ pours a glass and tries to help his father carefully sip.

Another cough helps Pastor Eli to clear his throat. "You mean to tell me that all I had to do to be in the same room with my son alone was to be rendered unconscious? I told you that even though the queen has convinced these women that we are their enemies, she would never allow them to mistreat us." Pastor Eli says.

Pastor Eli coughs again. "Take it easy old man. You need to rest. I want you to recover so that you can see me get married one day," EJ says wishfully. Pastor Eli allows the smile to fade from his face.

"Son, I want nothing more than to be at you and your brother's weddings. You both deserve that kind of happiness." EJ bows his head.

"I was only teasing father. We both know that marriage is against the women's law," EJ replied.

"It is not against GOD's law. This life of slavery is not a life that I envisioned for any of my children. You all deserve this kind of happiness that comes from sharing your life with someone who GOD blesses you with," Pastor Eli says.

EJ tries to clarify his father's statement. "Did you mean to say both of you?" That is when Pastor Eli pulls EJ close. "I meant what I said. I said exactly what I meant, son. I meant all of you," he says. EJ assumes that his father is speaking irrationally due to all the medication. "Father, do not stress yourself," EJ says.

"Promise me son. When GOD blesses you with a family that you have always dreamed of, you will be the father that you have always dreamed of. Don't make excuses. Fight for your family. Don't abandon them like I did. Don't turn your back on them for any reason." EJ nods even though he does not fully understand. "Your brother will not be the only sibling who needs you."

Males Are Not To Enter The Palace Unescorted...

Ezekiel wipes his hands on his pants to remove the debris from the window sill while Elizabeth makes the introductions. "Don't worry Mr. Shale. He is not a dangerous intruder. He is the one who helped Lliam escape. He was the one who took Eden." Then, she thought about what she said. "Wait a minute. That didn't exactly come out correctly."

Mr. Shale says, "It is alright. I know what you are trying to say. Besides, you said Eden is safe, unharmed and here. Thus, I guess I should be thanking you." Mr. Shale extends his hand to Ezekiel. He shakes it.

Ezekiel then asks, "She's here in this palace?"

"Yes!" she answers. "She told me to inform you, Mr. Shale, that you could help her find her grandmother while she seeks the queen." Mr. Shale is confused.

Enslaved By Family...

While withholding her tears, Eden refuses to lose eye contact with her cousin. Ilya steps aside to allow the guards to bind Eden's wrists and adhere a blindfold to her. At Vayl's command, Eden is escorted away while Amblin questions Ilya.

"Arresting Eden is beyond extreme, Ilya," Amblin says. She expresses how disturbed she is by her actions.

Visiting Hours Over...

EJ grips his father's hand. "Dad, what are you saying? Who are you talking about? Do I have another brother?" EJ asks.

Before Pastor Eli can answer, the power goes out. The alarm sounds, which prevents EJ from hearing the steel door to his hospital room being pushed open in the darkness. Within minutes, the alarm stops and the lights are restored. That is when EJ sees a face that he has longed to see. "Emil?" EJ asks. Emil and Lliam approach Pastor Eli's bedside. Emil and EJ embrace. "How did you know we were here?" EJ asks.

"Brothers do talk. Everyone is worried about father," Emil says as he moves in to hug him.

"How are you father?" Pastor Eli tearfully tells his beloved son that he has missed him. That is when Pastor Eli recognizes Lliam who is standing behind him. Pastor Eli is overjoyed and refers to Lliam as another son. That is when EJ recalls the question that his father had left unanswered prior to the power outage.

Emil warns that the guards will probably arrive soon, because they are responsible for the power outage. "We must move quickly to get you both out of here before they arrive. Then we must find Lliam's son."

EJ says, "Father is in no condition to travel."

"He is right, Emil," Pastor Eli attempts to say in the midst of coughing. "You three go without me. I will only slow you down. It is vital that you find the boy. I will pray for all of you." Pastor Eli begins to weaken in his ability to speak. The monitors begin to beep wildly. The guards can be heard in the corridor. Pastor Eli gathers enough strength to wish them well. "GOD will protect all of you, but you will need help from your sister." At these words, Pastor Eli becomes unconscious again.

They stand paralyzed at their father's announcement. They are not certain they heard him correctly. EJ aggressively tries to wake him. "Father! Father!"

Emil warns, "We must go now brother!"

Hidden Prisoners...

The guards guided Eden along familiar corridors within the palace. Eden recognized the smells and the changes in the ground underneath her feet. However, once they exited the palace and entered another building, her senses did not recognize where she was.

They walked along a very long corridor that carried a distinct echo. Eden tries to count the steps she takes. The guards halt. Eden tries to listen to their muffled conversation. Then, she feels fingers in the back of her head loosening the blindfold. The light hits Eden's eyes. Her vision is blurry. As her vision begins to clear, she sees glass walls that appear to be cells with women locked inside.

Vayl swipes her badge to open the glass door. The women inside immediately bow when they see Eden. She doesn't recognize any of them. Before Eden can ask them why they are there, she is injected with a tranquilizer.

Heal Thyself...

The guards heavily surround the entrance to Pastor Eli's hospital room. Ilya enters with her entourage. While the doctor completes documenting, Vayl informs Ilya about the escape of both of Pastor Eli's sons.

Ilya inquires about his condition. "His vitals are stable. He is having some difficulty with breathing due to his weakened heart, but he is conscious." Ilya excuses the physician to depart.

Ilya stands next to his bed. Pastor Eli can sense her anger with every breath she takes. "I will find your sons. And much like your beloved daughter, I will destroy them," Ilya vows. With tears, Pastor Eli gathers the strength to speak.

"You will never succeed in destroying all of my family, no matter how great your hate for me is," he gasps.

Ilya in anger turns to Vayl and Amblin. "Prepare the slaves the ceremony. Have them washed, dressed and counted. Then, prepare the male infants. It is time to teach these men that we will not tolerate their influence in our society. Let them weep over the deaths of their sons," Ilya states. Vayl agrees, but Amblin is disturbed.

From Above...

"He looks so peaceful. I miss him so much," Lliam says. EJ agrees as he and Lliam observe the baby through the vent in the ceiling at the hospital. It is quite a task for them to balance themselves on top of the beams.

Emil redirects. "Guys, we cannot remain here all night. We cannot get your son out of here right now. We need help." Lliam suddenly remembers. "You are right and I know just the person. We must get to the palace."

Wake Up...

Eden struggles to open her eyes. The glare from the sun is blinding. Her limbs feel heavy. She struggles to stand. As she tries to adjust her vision, she observes a small female child dressed in white. Eden tries to take steps towards the child, but the desert sand hinders her. She observes a second male child dressed also in white. She tries to speak.

Looking around, Eden realizes that there are numerous children surrounding her in the desert sand as far as her eyes can see. She blinks to clear the grains of sand from her eyelashes so that she can focus. She begins to feel gentle small fingers take hold of her hand. She looks down her arm to find a small boy dressed in white.

The boy begins to guide her steps. Eden is able to walk with ease through the sand without sinking. The heat combined with the powerful glare of the sun causes Eden to hallucinate. She assumes that she is seeing a mirage of a river. As she and the boy approach, they see a male soldier at the river's edge. He is dressed in militaristic uniform yielding a striking double-edged sword. He is cradling an infant male. Eden sees the soldier throw the baby into the river. She tries to scream when she sees a crocodile swim towards the baby, but she is unable. The vision fades. The boy disappears.

Eden uncovers her eyes to see another child, a small girl. The child is dressed in heavy wool coat. It is dark and cold where she is standing. She is surrounded by massive trees with no leaves.

As Eden's feet sink deep into the snowy tundra terrain, Eden quickly makes her approach beside the girl. Once Eden reaches the girl, she bends down to examine the child whose blue eyes are filled with tears. There is a large six-pointed star loosely attached to her sleeve. Eden also sees what appears to be a pool of blood layering the snow.

Drop by drop, the blood falls onto them like rain. Eden is almost too afraid to look up. She steps away from the child and reaches out to touch the trunks of the trees. It is difficult to see in the dark night air. The moon is the only source of light. Eden places her fingers onto the tree only to notice that the tree is made entirely of metal. Suddenly, Eden's heart beats rapidly as she slowly backs away from the tree and the child.

Before she can fully make sense of what is happening, she is instantly surrounded by Nazi soldiers. One by one, the soldiers are executing children by throwing them onto the metal branches made to look like trees. Eden forces herself to look up only to find their small bodies mangled amidst the limbs. Their blood drops into the snow below.

Eden is shaking. Her eyes widen when she hears more screams. She looks behind her. There are several older children and teens standing silently before her. All of them have black skin that glistens in blood. Eden walks among them. They part to allow her to pass. Suddenly, swarms of young black girls rush past her. Dressed in school uniforms, they are screaming and bleeding. That is when Eden sees the male boys running towards her with machetes. Eden holds up her arms to stop one of the boys. A young woman dressed in white grasps both of her hands.

When Eden looks up, she is suddenly holding an infant in her arms. She is of Asian descent. Eden cradles the child and watches her smile. Eden takes a deep breath when she suddenly feels a gun against her head. "Get up!" a male voice orders. Eden is forced to walk towards a shipping container. The gate on the container is hoisted open revealing many females in shackles. Eden screams, "No!"

Eden drops to her knees, broken with terror. She cries loudly. The woman dressed in white stands before her with a small boy standing beside her. She wipes Eden's tears and says, "GOD shares your tears. But now it is time for you to wake up and stop these acts of evil before the wrath of GOD is pronounced. Wake up Eden!"

Eden opens her eyes. She still thinks that she is dreaming because she sees a familiar face of a person from her past who is supposed to be dead looking at her. "Eden, wake up!" Eden responds as she reaches out to touch her face, "Nanny Vivian? You are alive?"

Much Needed Discussion...

Amblin paces back and forth inside Ilya's private quarters, listening to Vayl and Ilya talk. "Are we to prepare for executions of the slaves or infants? It has been years since the last execution. The queen vehemently opposed them without cause," Vayl reminded.

Ilya replied, "Grandmother did find such events barbaric."

Amblin gathered the courage to also speak. "Your grandmother was right. Forgive me Ilya. I love you with all of my heart and I would do anything for you, but you have gone too far. You are talking about killing innocent children. You even want to kill Eden." Amblin asserts. "I don't understand. I don't understand what you are thinking. I certainly don't understand what you are doing. I thought you simply wanted to make a statement to Eden. I thought you wanted to let Eden know that you should lead. Now, you want to kill without reason. This is savage behavior that I would expect out of the males which is the very reason your grandmother had them enslaved. Have you forgotten?"

Ilya tries to withhold her frustration and persuade Amblin to understand that these actions are to advance their new world. "We must rid ourselves of sympathizers. If Eden were to rule, this citadel would return to male dominance and male violence. You must trust that I am putting every woman's best interest first."

Ilya attempts to pacify Amblin with a hug. She asks a nurse to administer a sedative to Amblin to help her rest.

What Plan...

"Did she say how long it would take her?" Ezekiel asks. Elizabeth shakes her head. Mr. Shale expresses his concern regarding Eden's search for the queen.

"It should not take her this long. Eden has access to her grandmother's quarters," Mr. Shale says, but Elizabeth and Ezekiel are confused. Ezekiel asks, "Why does her grandmother reside in the queen's palace?"

Mr. Shale realizes why they are confused. "The queen is her grandmother. Eden is royalty. All that time you spent together, she never told you?" Mr. Shale says.

Ezekiel shakes his head in bewilderment. Mr. Shale responds, "Eden is very modest. She does not speak much, but she observes everything. She is quite the opposite of her cousin, Princess Ilya." Ezekiel and Elizabeth remain speechless at this news. However, it occurs to Mr. Shale at that moment that her cousin may be the reason for Eden's detainment.

Hidden Prisoners...

Eden is confused about where she is and who these women are. Eden stares at Ms. Vivian. She is pleasantly surprised to see that aside from a few streaks of gray hair, Ms. Vivian has not aged one bit. "I thought you were dead. I don't understand," she says.

Ms. Vivian sits next to Eden and begins to explain. "We have all been imprisoned here for having a difference in opinion. Your cousin placed me here many years ago. It is complicated." Eden asks, "Does grandmother know that you are here?"

Ms. Vivian replies, "I don't know if your grandmother knows that this place exists. This building was designed to be a private training academy for elite students of law, policy, languages and history. But, your grandmother did not feel it would be fair to classify and rank the girls. She felt that comparisons and competition were degrading and promoted division. She had the building sealed. Your cousin, on the other hand, has fostered the spirit of competition since she was born. And you have been her biggest rival."

"Ilya placed you here? But, Ilya loves you. You raised us. You are not our enemy," Eden says. Then Ms. Vivian looks around at the other imprisoned women before she replies, "I used to believe that too."

"Over the years, Ilya has placed us all here for either speaking against the system or for committing the worst crime of all," Ms. Vivian admits.

Eden stares at Ms. Vivian's face in amazement at how smooth it still was. She still had a perfect smile that caused her nose to wrinkle. Eden reaches to hold Ms. Vivian's hands. Then Eden asks, "Did you all give birth to males?" Ms. Vivian shakes her head in disagreement. Ms. Vivian answers, "Actually, we all fell in love with a male." Eden quietly reserves her reaction. Instead, she observes all the different faces of the women in the cell with her.

Laundry Room Haven...

"Can't we just go get her?" Ezekiel asks. Mr. Shale and Elizabeth look at one another in disbelief. Mr. Shale then reminds Ezekiel that he is lucky to be alive and standing in the palace. Elizabeth laughs.

"I think we will need a more concrete plan to find her. This citadel is enormous. The princess could have had Eden taken anywhere. I guess we should start by trying to gain access to the queen's private quarters. It is the middle of the night. Everyone should be sleeping," Mr. Shale says.

On the Roof...

"It is getting cold," EJ says, hovering next to the generators on the hospital rooftop. Lliam promises, "Patience my friend, we won't be out here too long. I just need to see what is happening at the palace," he says while looking down below through his night-vision binoculars.

EJ asks, "May I ask where you got binoculars from? In fact, you have an entire arsenal here."

Lliam and Emil look at one another and oddly respond in unison, "Don't ask."

EJ warns, "You both had better hope that no one is observing us right now."

"Gentlemen, there is something here that deserves our attention," Lliam says. EJ and Emil rush to his side to see what it is. "A slave is being taken into the Palace."

"At this time of night?" EJ exclaims. Lliam hands the binoculars to Emil who confirms the report. He asks, "Why would a slave be brought to the palace at this hour?" They decide to find out.

Mandatory Meeting...

Ilya stands in the doorway, observing Amblin resting in her quarters. The door slides closed. Ilya turns to Vayl and asks, "Is the slave here?" Vayl confirms and guides her down the corridor.

They make their way to the lower level of the palace by the laundry facility. Ilya asks Vayl, "Have the guards stand by." Ilya, then, enters the room. Nealon bows. Ilya stands before him while he continues to bow. She places her hand on his forehead. Then, she slides her hand down to his cheek. "Rise!" She orders. Nealon stands upright. He towers over her with his tall slender frame. He cautiously moves closer to her and kisses her. They embrace.

"I am so sorry that I failed you. I know you wanted your cousin gone, but it is not easy for me to kill. I know that you think that it is, but you are wrong," Nealon explains. Ilya releases herself from their embrace and places her hands gently on his cheeks.

"I know I have not done much to refute the reputation that I have gained. But, despite what everyone thinks, I am not a murderer. You know that, yet you want me to harm your cousin. Why? I don't understand," he says.

Ilya takes a deep breath in frustration. Before she can answer, Nealon further explains, "I was young and stupid when I caused that woman's death. But you know it was an accident," Nealon insists. Ilya quiets him and says, "I know that this is hard for you."

"You could not complete the task of harming her because you actually do have a heart. I have known that about you since we were kids. Unlike me, you care. It also did not help that you saw the son of the woman you were accused of killing," Ilya states as Nealon lowers his head.

Nealon grabs Ilya's hands. "I just want to be forgiven. I want to forget the past and this place. I want you to leave with me. This place is destroying you and us. We are not these people. We can be better people if we simply leave. Let's start over somewhere far away from here. I promise to take care of you. You know that I would do anything for you. I love you," He confesses.

Ilya releases her hands from his grip and turns away and says, "Love is a luxury no male could ever understand and no woman could ever afford to believe in."

Owed An Apology...

Eden is at a loss for words after hearing how each woman became enslaved. She tries to make sense of it. "Why would Ilya do this? Why would she imprison other women? We are supposed to be more than a community. Why would she imprison the woman who raised us?" Eden asks as she looks at Ms. Vivian. She becomes angry at realizing what her cousin has done.

Ms. Vivian tries to provide an answer. "I wish I could explain, but even after all of these years it would be impossible to make sense of it all. I can assure you that if you were to search our records you would probably find that we are all classified as "deceased" at the instruction of your cousin."

Eden places her head down. Ms. Vivian says, "Despite Ilya's behaviors and choices, it is not about her. Ilya was as much a victim of the sins of men as we all were."

Ms. Vivian continues, "The men were never Ilya's greatest enemy. Her pride was. She was always desperate for your grandmother's and your mother's approval. For her, their approval equaled love. I think you and I got in her way. It was hard to see that we are all in the same sinking ship, males and females."

Ms. Vivian says, "Please know that your grandmother was extremely brave to establish this new world. She did so for a very good reason. The men were causing great destruction. And women needed protection. Enslaving the males was her solution to resolving the ills of this complicated world. But, this social experiment that was far from ideal. We need the males as much as they need us." Eden is stunned at these words.

Ms. Vivian says, "I know that this is hard for you to hear, but my years of imprisonment have given me clarity. Ilya needed a reliable male in her life. She needed her father. He was the one person whose love would have drastically changed her. It still can."

Eden asks in confusion, "Her father?"

Laundry Sanctuary...

The weight of the cart causes the wheels to squeak. Nevertheless, Mr. Shale maneuvers the laundry cart through the corridor. He maintains minimal eye contact with the guards. Yet, one of the guards catches his attention. "Mr. Shale, you never cease to amaze me with your loyalty to the queen. Here it is late in the night and you are still serving. You make us all look lazy," she smiled. Mr. Shale replied, "Serving the queen is my honor, ma'am." The guard bids Mr. Shale a good night and allows him to proceed towards the queen's quarters.

Another guard greets Mr. Shale at the entrance. She reminds Mr. Shale that the queen is still recovering. As he observes the queen sleeping, he replies, "Yes ma'am." The guard then exits. Mr. Shale maneuvers the laundry cart past the bathroom and inside the queen's closet. He taps the side of the cart twice before he departs.

Inside The Palace...

"For such a late hour, there seems to be much activity occurring inside the palace," EJ says.

"Where would they take a slave at this hour. All the royals should be sleeping. I am certain we saw a slave coming this way. He must be here somewhere," Emil says as they make their way into the engineering room of the palace.

Startled By Voices...

"Could you be any louder?" Elizabeth asks Ezekiel. He helps her out of the laundry cart. Elizabeth dusts herself while Ezekiel explores the enormous bathroom and dressing room. "Royals know how to live," Ezekiel says as he sniffs the garments hanging in the queen's closet. He is captivated by the scent of her perfume.

Elizabeth redirects his attention to the door leading to queen's bedroom. However, they are interrupted by the sound of nearby voices. They quickly dim the lights and hide. Elizabeth can hear the voices echoing through the air vents in the wall. Neither is surprised to hear a female voice. Yet, Ezekiel is stunned that the second voice sounds so familiar. It is a male voice. They listen very carefully to the conversation.

Sacrifice Of A Slave...

Nealon wraps his arms around Ilya. "We were kids together. It was the war that divided us. You grew to become a beautiful princess. I grew to become foolish and full of anger. I was just as much a victim of the war as you. But despite what your grandmother filled your head with, you showed me mercy. You believed in me. That is how I know that you love me," he insists. He cradles her face. "You know I would do anything for you. Don't deny us. We can leave this place and never look back. We can start over and be free of both of our crimes. Just say yes," Nealon pleads.

"I cannot. This is my destiny." Ilya states.

"Do you think that these women will not realize what we have done? Neither of us will ever be able to deceive them for long," Nealon states.

Ilya replies, "My grandmother was not entirely wrong. I cannot let any male infant be born into this land and destroy all that we have built. Our land is now safe from the violence of males. Can't you see that?"

"But for how long Ilya? You have adopted the exact same ideology of violence simply to gain control and power. If you stay, if you continue in this mindset, you will be no different from any other tyrannical leader in every war throughout history. You want the same power that every male-dominated society has strived for."

With tears in her eyes, Ilya tightly hugs Nealon. She whispers, "I do love you, but you will never understand." She injects him with a drug and watches him fall to the floor. She exits. The door slides closed behind her.

Ilya finds Vayl standing in the hallway with the guards. She informs Vayl that she will be in her quarters resting. "Tomorrow will be eventful."

Unexpected Rescue...

Eden maintains a whisper so as not to wake the other female prisoners. She asks, "Where is my grandmother?" Ms. Vivian states, "The queen has fallen ill. We don't know any details. That is what we heard from a sympathetic guard."

Eden paces in worry. Before they can further their conversation, they hear the heavy door to the outside open. Footsteps approach. Ms. Vivian and Eden quickly lie down, close their eyes and pretend to be sleeping.

Eden squints to open one eye. She can see the frame of a slender, short woman through the glass. She hears the beep from the security system. The door slides open. The footsteps approach. Eden anxiously senses a presence hovering above her.

Eden feels a cold hand on her shoulder. She tries to remain calm. A voice whispers, "Wake up!" Eden slowly opens her eyes. She tries to control her surprise. "Amblin?" Eden says.

"I must get you out of here," Amblin says. Eden is speechless. Amblin reaches for her hand, but Eden hesitates. Amblin realizes Eden's resistance and says, "Eden, I cannot apologize enough for what we have done to you. I don't expect you to trust me. I did not realize what Ilya's plan was until you were already in danger."

Amblin continues. "I love Ilya, but I also love you. You are both my family. I know that I have always been closer to Ilya, but I would have never allowed you to be hurt and betrayed like this. I cannot apologize enough. I am truly sorry. Please believe me."

Eden then shakes Ms. Vivian. Ms. Vivian sits up. Amblin recognizes her. Ms. Vivian greets her. Amblin seems surprised to see her. Eden asks Amblin how long had she known that this prison for the women existed. Amblin replies, "Not as long as you might think. Trust me when I say that I had no idea that Ms. Vivian was here."

Ms. Vivian states, "She may be telling the truth. I have never seen her down here."

Just Before Dawn...

The sky begins to lighten. Emil opens his eyes to find EJ sleeping beside him. He sits up and looks around the engineering room. He sees Lliam sitting at a desk reading under a brightly-lit lamp.

He rises to stretch and approaches Lliam. He sees blueprints and books on computer engineering before Lliam. "What is all of this?" Emil asks. Lliam studies the designs of the various buildings and the intricacies of the computer system. He responds, "This may all be our keys to the kingdom, literally."

Inside The Cell...

The women are dressing and preparing themselves for their release while Amblin and Eden talk. Ms. Vivian approaches Eden and Amblin. She says, "The last time that I saw you two together like this, you were little girls. You were both so happy and united then." Eden and Amblin look at one another and smile.

Ms. Vivian continues. "One thing has not changed. I knew that Eden would bring about change and hope. You brought it in the midst of the war we endured the way that you cared for our refugees and injured. Now, you are bringing change for our future."

Eden inhales deeply. Amblin nods in agreement. Ms. Vivian states, "As a child, you tried to free some fish that had been caught. You could not stand the idea of those fish being trapped in a net instead of living in their home in the sea. You not only set them free. You were so bothered at the injustice of their capture that you refused to eat for days in protest. You did that at age five." Eden smiled.

Ms. Vivian continues to tell her that she has always known Eden to value life. "That is the essence of who you are. You are very much like your mother. She had a huge heart for people and causes too."

Ms. Vivian continues, "The intentions of your mother and grandmother established this society ruled by women. I was the greatest supporter of their mission. Yet, much like the brutality of the men went against GOD, so did their good intentions." Amblin and Eden nod while Ms. Vivian states, "You may have been taught that males are dangerous and unpredictable. We all have. But, we need each other to survive."

Eden responds. "Even if I get out of this cell or locate this baby, I still don't exactly know what I can do."

Ms. Vivian insists. "You do what GOD has already placed inside of you to do. I know the word "GOD" scares you, but you must do whatever it takes. You defend and protect the innocent. You speak truth. You hope. You show courage, wisdom, and compassion. This is not the time to question what you have learned. This is the time to act."

Eden briefly recalls her time spent with Ezekiel in the woods and how he protected her. For the first time, the memory of him stirs her heart.

One of the female prisoners interrupts Ms. Vivian to announce that the ladies are ready. Eden looks into the faces of all the ladies with admiration and tears. Amblin begins to instruct the ladies regarding their escape. Eden turns toward Ms. Vivian and asks, "You know who my father is, don't you?" Ms. Vivian nods affirmatively before she says, "You are very much like him." Eden smiles.

Awkward Awakening...

She can hear his heart beating as she buries herself in his chest. The warmth of his body allows her to sleep soundly. For the first time in months, Elizabeth feels tremendous peace and comfort as she rests in the quietness of the queen's closet. It does not take long for reality to set in when she is awakened by Ezekiel coughing. She quickly rises and moves away from him.

She looks around the room. Every article of clothing smells so clean. She looks back at Ezekiel sleeping. She decides to explore the dressing room. She searches through drawers and cabinets.

Elizabeth locates an opening in the wall that is seemingly sealed. She pushes around the seam to create a break in the seal. Ezekiel continues to sleep. She enters through the opening and finds the steel ladder. She climbs to the bottom of the ladder in the darkness. She feels along the wall and finds a switch. The lights come on, revealing a hidden corridor.

Cautiously, she proceeds. The corridor is cold and dim. She makes her way into a room that is full with the activity of computers, monitors and security systems. She approaches a desk and touches the chair realizing it is warm. Her heart begins to race. She is not alone.

As she turns to run, someone grabs her forearm. A hand covers her mouth, blocking her scream.

Escape Route...

Footsteps move along the dimly lit corridor. The females follow Amblin out of the cell. As the women hurry, Eden inquires of Amblin. "How do you plan to release these female prisoners who have been declared deceased?"

Amblin replies, "My original intent was to release only you. Your cousin has planned a government event for this morning which would provide enough of a distraction. However, I had no idea I would be embodying the very spirit of Harriett Tubman right now. I had not planned a mass escape. Therefore, I will welcome any suggestion you may have." Eden looks towards Ms. Vivian for help. But, Ms. Vivian only laughs.

Then, Ms. Vivian offers a possible solution to Amblin. She devises a plan to divide the women. Eden interrupts Ms. Vivian, "I trust that you both can get these women to safety while I find my grandmother. Don't worry about me. I will join you both soon," Eden says before she departs from the group.

How Is The Patient...

The door slides open and the physician enters the hospital room. "Any changes?" she asks. The nurse shows the doctor Pastor's Eli vitals and responds. "He is stable."

The physician reviews the electronic chart. They quietly depart.

The beeps from the monitors dominate the room. Pastor Eli tries to wake himself from the sedative, but his eye lids are heavy. As he begins to surrender to his drowsiness, he can hear the door to his room open once more. Footsteps draw closer to his bed and stop. He struggles to open his eyes. He can feel a hand on his shoulder. "I hope that you can hear me because I need your help, my friend." It is Mr. Shale.

Males Are To Be Quarantined...

"Princess Ilya, what are you doing here so early? You went to bed just a few hours ago. Did you get any sleep?" Vayl asks. Ilya stood before her in the lobby of the infant male unit. She appears refreshed and dressed in a metallic gold-trimmed royal robe. "I am good."

Ilya inquired of Vayl. "Have the guards prepared all the slaves for this morning's events?" Vayl replies, "All has been prepared according to your instructions. "That will be all for now," Ilya says as she dismisses Vayl.

Ilya then enters the infant male unit. Faint beeping of monitors can be heard. She walks by each incubator and views the infant males until she stops at the crib of Elizabeth and Lliam's baby. She finds herself intrigued as she stares at him. His face is angelic.

It does not take long for her to notice the distinct birthmark on his foot. Ilya moves closer to the child. When she leans over him in an effort to touch him, his birthmark begins to glow in brilliance. In fear, she retreats. She tries to gather herself by removing the sweat from her brow. She quickly exits the room and retrieves a guard. She requests that they begin to prepare the male infants as well for the morning event.

Not The Same...

Eden maneuvers through the palace which is abnormally quiet. She enters her grandmother's room and makes her way into her grandmother's private study. The sweet fragrance of her office generates memories and tears.

She browses the library of discs, videos and texts references. The categories disturb her. "Ageism, AIDS, abortions, abuse, alcoholism, bullying, bankruptcy, kidnapping, larceny, lynching, Nazism molestation, murder, pornography, prostitution, racism, rape, slavery, sociopath, terrorism, trafficking..."

She closes her eyes in disgust before turning her attention to her grandmother's desk. She admires the display of family photos. She opens a drawer to find a photo of her mother standing next to a gentleman with two little boys. They seem oddly familiar. As she struggles to remember, she hears a cough. In fear, Eden quickly hides under the desk. The coughing continues. After holding her breath, she slowly emerges from beneath the desk to investigate.

She follows the sound into the bedroom where the coughing seems more intense. As she moves closer to the bed, she finds her grandmother. Eden is appalled at the sight of her. Covered heavily in blankets, this once statuesque ruler appears frail and weak.

Flight or Fight...

Elizabeth can feel her heart racing as she struggles to free herself from the grip of her unseen assailant. The hand covering her mouth is suffocating. A heavy voice whispers sternly into her ear. "Do not scream. It's me." Elizabeth is paralyzed briefly. The grip over her mouth lessens allowing her to turn around and confirm the voice that she seems to recognize. "Lliam!" she says in relief. They embrace.

"What are you doing here?" she says. Before Lliam can answer, EJ and Emil emerge from hiding. Lliam then states, "I guess you could say damage control."

Last Words...

With her head wrapped in bandages, the queen reaches for Eden. Eden kneels by her bedside to comfort her grandmother and takes her hand. The queen can barely speak. Eden is careful not to disturb the secured electrodes or the IV. Eden begins to speak, but the queen stops her when she reaches up to place her fingertips on Eden's lips. Eden is overwhelmed. The poor physical condition of her grandmother reminds Eden of the final moments spent with her mother.

Eden is at a loss for words. Her grandmother whispers, "Please let me speak. I have few words and less time. I love you and your cousin. I'm sorry I failed you."

Eden interrupts. "Grandmother, that couldn't be further from the truth."

The queen struggles to speak through her coughing. Eden retrieves water for her, but the queen grasps Eden's hand. "I lied to you both. I wanted to protect you, but I was only protecting myself," the queen says. Eden tries to stop her grandmother from overexerting herself. "Grandmother, we can talk about this later."

"No!" The queen snaps. She begins to cough again.

The queen continues, "You need the truth. You need your father!" The queen insists. Eden frowns in silence. Her grandmother pulls her close. They stare at one another. Eden observes her grandmother's eyes widening and her breath becoming shallow. "Your father will help you. Please forgive me." The queen pleads as she closes her eyes.

Her body goes limp and a tear falls. Eden begins to tremble. She tightly embraces her grandmother and tells her to hold on. Eden presses her ear against her grandmother's chest, but hears no heartbeat. She screams out for help. She no longer cares if any guards capture her. She attempts to revive her grandmother. There is no response. She squeezes her grandmother's body and cries out again for help. Trembling, she cannot let her grandmother go. Her mind begins to be flooded with images of her mother. She is so distressed that she does not notice the hand resting on her shoulder.

Eden refuses to open her eyes. She refuses to face the pain in this moment. It is in this moment that she can hardly breathe. Before she can fully absorb the reality of this moment, she recognizes a reassuring voice. It is a strong, deep and soothing voice that gently commands her to let her grandmother go. She finds the will to look up. Through her tears, she realizes it is Ezekiel. He is extending his hand to her. Her pain is so great that she desperately reaches out to grasp his hand. He holds her tightly and allows her to cry deeply in his arms.

Call to Pre-order...

Ilya stands before the balcony overlooking the frenzy below. She absorbs the warmth of the sun and the energy of the crowd. The colorful flags of the citadel wave boldly above the arena. She contemplates her private thoughts in silence. Those thoughts are interrupted by Vayl.

"Pardon me, Princess Ilya." She says. "The slaves have been prepared. They will be escorted into the arena at your command." Ilya nods in approval.

"Make sure Amblin is ready for the processional," Ilya says. Vayl says that she has not seen Amblin all morning.

Undercover Big Brother...

Elizabeth notifies them of the crowd gathering outside. "I can lead you all to the queen's quarters," Elizabeth insists. Emil agrees. "She is right. We cannot stay hidden any longer."

Lliam interrupts. He motions for EJ, Emil and Elizabeth to join him in front of the security monitors. They all view the male slaves being shackled into single file lines. "What is happening?" EJ asks.

Not Much Time...

A smile gently emerges on Pastor Eli's face as he lays eyes on his old loyal friend. "Are you in any pain?" Mr. Shale asks Pastor Eli.

Pastor Eli responds, "I am tougher than that." They both grin. Pastor Eli swallows to clear his throat. He says, "I am guessing that you fought your way to be by my side for a reason. I can see it in your eyes my friend. You had that very same determination during the war."

Mr. Shale reaches to take Pastor Eli's hand. It is cold and trembling. He holds it tight to steady it. Pastor Eli says, "When we were in college together, do you remember all the protesting we did?" Mr. Shale laughs in response.

Pastor Eli says, "We fought so much against the establishment that I kept forgetting which issues belonged to which cause. To this day, I still have to talk myself into supporting anything." Mr. Shale continues to laugh in agreement and says, "The crazy part was that you were part of the establishment, man! Your father governed the country for goodness sake." They laugh.

Pastor Eli coughs a bit and says, "Remember how we always dreamed of becoming judges. We were going to change the world." Mr. Shale removes the tears from his eyes and nods. Suddenly, Pastor Eli's voice becomes serious in tone. "You never could hide anything from me old friend. You have always been a man of few words. Yet, your words were always truthful and impacting."

Mr. Shale does his best to carefully select his words. He is well aware that Pastor Eli's health is failing. He says, "There is still time for us to change the world. We can do that through your children." Mr. Shale pauses before he states, "Your daughter desperately needs you."

Pastor Eli closes his eyes briefly and asks, "Which one?"

Even Less Time...

Ezekiel pulls her hair back and gently wipes her tears. "We must get out of here. The guards will be here soon." Ezekiel helps lift her to her feet.

He holds her hand to guide her out of the room. He can feel her resisting. He looks back to see her lean over her grandmother. She removes a necklace from her grandmother's neck and places it on herself. Then, Eden kisses her grandmother's forehead and covers her with a blanket. They depart.

Front Row Seat...

EJ, Emil, Elizabeth and Lliam are locked in front of the security monitors. "There is no way they are preparing for any celebration. Is the queen preparing a public execution?" EJ asks. "There must be something that we can do," Elizabeth says.

They continue to watch as the males are being marched into the arena. They are secured in electronic shackles.

Elizabeth becomes so nervous that she places her hand over her mouth. Emil starts to pace.

EJ states, "Dad always told us to have faith in GOD. He always provides a way. I do not believe these women hate all males. There must be a way to reach their hearts and free our brothers."

Looking around, EJ finds the security panel for the male containment units at the prison. He realizes that the units and the electronic bands could be short-circuited.

Face to Face...

Eden tries to focus on following Ezekiel along the corridors within the palace. They can hear the guards approaching. They search for a place to hide and stumble into a hidden area behind her cousin's private quarters. They hold their breath in an effort to silence themselves until the guards clear.

While Ezekiel listens through the door, another sound captures Eden's attention. It is the sound of someone gasping. She realizes they are no longer alone. Cautiously, she turns around to see a male slave lying breathlessly on the floor. She immediately recognizes him as the one who attacked her in the woods. She draws back in fear.

Immediately, she alerts Ezekiel. When he sees Nealon's face, his rage instantly surfaces. Eden senses that Ezekiel is about to attack the slave. Yet, when she returns her attention to the slave, she realizes that he is severely injured. She rises quickly to stop Ezekiel from charging him. "No!" she yells.

Ezekiel breathes hard. Eden instantly cautions, "Something is wrong. He is injured." Eden nears and kneels by his side to examine him. Ezekiel warns. "You cannot trust him! He is the one who killed my mother!"

Eden continues to engage him. "Are you hurt?" She asks. He nods. She tries to help him sit up. He is shivering. She looks to Ezekiel to help, but he refuses to come near.

She then tries to wipe his brow and calm him. "What is your name?" She asks. "It's Nealon," he gasps. "Please help me." He begs Eden. She seeks to comfort him. She asks, "What happened?" Nealon wraps his arms around his body writhing in pain. "It is getting worse," he says.

"What is?" Eden asks. "The poison," he replies. Nealon points to the discarded vial and a syringe. Eden is confused. She does know that poisoning a slave is not a customary form of punishment in their kingdom. Thus, she asks, "Who poisoned you?"

As Nealon struggles to answer, Eden asserts, "We must get you to the hospital before you die." Nealon then grabs her arm while she is holding him. He warns her, "There is no time."

Nealon confesses. "I know what I have done. I committed horrible crimes. But you must believe me when I say that I did not kill that woman many years ago. It was an accident. I have never killed anyone, but I knew that no one would ever believe me. Even that day in the woods, I could not take your life no matter how much the princess wanted me too." Eden is in shock at hearing this confession.

Nealon continues. "I thought I could. Everyone already labeled me as a killer. I love the princess. I would do anything for her. She wanted you gone, but I just could not kill you." Eden simply shook her head.

Nealon further admits, "I have been in love with her since we were children." Eden found this news surprising. Nealon grins. "I sacrificed my freedom to become a slave. I did that to be with her."

Nealon's breathing gradually slows. "I begged her to leave this place with me and start a new life. I wanted her to love me as much as I love her. The princess told me that men don't have the capacity to love. Try telling my heart that." Ezekiel draws closer to hear the rest of Nealon's confession.

Nealon then says, "I suppose now I will be free of my sins through death." At this, Ezekiel hung his head. Nealon tries to focus on Ezekiel. "I know I hurt you. I would do anything to undo the damage that I have caused both of you. I beg of you to forgive me. One day I hope that you will."

Eden stared at Ezekiel. The cheering of a crowd could be heard coming from outside. Eden is alarmed. She looks down at Nealon who is cradled in her arms and tries to offer him a look of forgiveness with a smile. "If I had not loved Ilya so much, I would not be dying now. But, I also would not be on my way to freedom." Eden tries to withhold tears.

Nealon asks for a favor. "Please forgive Ilya. Please forgive me. And please tell her that I love her still. Do not allow her to destroy anyone else, including herself." He closes his eyes and breathes his last.

In The Face...

The council hall is full with royals and officials. They converse without direction. No one is certain what to expect at the morning ceremonies.

Before Ilya can make her way into the hall, Vayl demands her attention. They enter the private administrative headquarters. Ilya moves about the room in nervousness while the steel doors slide shut.

Vayl watches Ilya as she rambles and moves. "As soon as this ends, I must share the events of this ceremony with grandmother."

Ilya stands still long enough to notice that Vayl is being unusually silent. Vayl tries to find the words, but her voice breaks. "Please sit down," she says. Ilya is slow in heeding the direction, but she eventually sits. Vayl announces, "Our queen, your grandmother, is gone." Vayl can no longer speak. Ilya stoically rises. Then she turns away from Vayl and looks out the window. In that moment, she refuses to feel. Devoid any hint of upset, Ilya turns and says, "It is time."

Divide and Conquer...

While EJ and Lliam devise a plan to short circuit the bands on the slaves, Elizabeth and Emil search for communication devices. The sound of panic from Lliam instantly draws them to what is occurring on the screens.

Elizabeth cries out, "My GOD, no!" They all watch as the infant males are paraded onto the platform. Elizabeth grabs Lliam's arm. They look into each other's eyes instantly communicating their shared distress. "You have got to go save our son," she urges. He nods.

Lliam turns to Emil. "Say the word. I am with you," Emil affirms. Lliam begins to bark commands. "EJ, stay here and continue working on the system. Elizabeth, help EJ."

Elizabeth contends. "Please let me go with you. He's my son too." Lliam hugs Elizabeth to calm her down.

Then, he asks, "Do you trust me?" Elizabeth nods. Lliam says, "I need you to trust me now more than ever."

To The Arena...

Eden changes into military gear that she finds in Ilya's quarters. She returns to the room where Ezekiel is still hiding. He is disturbed at the initial sight of her. Eden asks, "What do you think?" He just shakes his head.

She insists, "I am certain that I can get us into the arena. I just need a little help from my personal slave." Ezekiel is initially unsure what she means. Then, he realizes that she is speaking about him.

Pomp and Circumstance...

Ilya enters into the arena greeted by thunderous applause and a standing ovation. The energy from the crowd allows her to hide her grief. She returns a majestic wave before she takes to the throne elevated high above the arena floor. The moment is bittersweet.

The ceremony begins with formal music and grandiose speech from the senator of the citadel while Ilya looks on. The governor of the council rises to make an announcement. Ilya is very much lost in her thoughts. She can hear the governor speak, but she is unable to concentrate. Her thoughts are haunted by the voice of her grandmother and Nealon.

Slaves are paraded onto the floor in shackles in front of the all-female crowd. Ilya is so distracted by her two recent losses that she does not hear the formal announcement made to the citizens regarding her new role as leader.

Common Sense Enemy...

Eden escorts Ezekiel through the densely populated female crowd inside the arena while trying not to attract any attention from the guards. "You know you would have made an ideal personal slave," she teases. Ezekiel simply shakes his head and redirects, "Would you focus." He demands.

They observe the presence of the heavy security throughout the arena. Eden immediately locates Ilya positioned high above the crowd. She is seated in their grandmother's seat. She alerts Ezekiel. The noise of the crowd makes it difficult for them to hear one another.

Ezekiel tries to direct her path forward. They attempt to move unnoticed, but fail. Before they reach the floor of the arena, Ezekiel and Eden are apprehended by several female guards dressed in hoods. Without uttering a sound, they are blindfolded and led away from the crowd. Eden is unfamiliar with the path they are taking. She senses that they must have been taken to some sort of chamber because she recognizes the heavy squeak in the swing of the metal door.

They both try to adjust their vision with the removal of their blindfolds. But it is the sound of a very familiar voice that brings relief to Eden. One of the hooded women says, "You two have caused a tremendous amount of trouble." Eden frowns in confusion as the woman continues. I only hope that we can live with ourselves considering what we are about to do. And you two better be worth the sacrifice," the woman says as she removes her hood. It is Ms. Vivian. Eden hugs her in excitement. Amblin removes her hood as well.

The Key...

Elizabeth prays while EJ works diligently to access the mainframe. In the middle of her prayer, Elizabeth hears footsteps. She instructs EJ to continue working. "Whoever it is, I will distract them," she says. EJ agrees.

She exits the engineering room and strategically hides along the corridor to prepare for action. She hears footsteps approaching. She holds her breath in anticipation. As soon as the person gets close, Elizabeth lunges. They both fall. There is not much of a fight because Mr. Shale raises his arms in submission.

Time To Rule...

Before Ilya is able to address the crowd, cheers ring out in support of her leadership. Ilya withholds tears. This is the moment she has dreamed of. She takes it all in as she prepares herself to accept her new role.

Ilya waves in response to the applause of the crowd. She attempts to speak. "It is with honor and respect that I accept your support. I will continue my grandmother's legacy and lead all of you into a bright future. You deserve dignity and our girls deserve a greater quality of life."

In Disguise...

The guards command that the men rise to their feet. Their shackles are inspected and secured. "Here is one more," Ms. Vivian states while keeping her face hidden beneath her hood. She hands Ezekiel over to the guards to be shackled and transferred. The last of the slaves proceed into the arena.

Combining Efforts...

Elizabeth removes herself from atop Mr. Shale. "Are you okay? I am terribly sorry!" Elizabeth apologizes. Mr. Shale tries to assure her by redirecting her attention to his question. "How did you end up down here?"

Suddenly, Elizabeth remembers EJ. She grasps Mr. Shale's hand and gently tries to help him rise. She is mindful of his disabled arm. She urges, "Follow me!"

EJ becomes very nervous when he sees Elizabeth reentering the engineering room with an elderly man. Mr. Shale calls his name, "Eli Junior". Instantly, EJ stands and says, "Mr. Shale." They embrace.

Elizabeth watches their reunion while waiting for one of them to offer her an explanation as to how they know one another. EJ wipes his tears and tells Elizabeth that Mr. Shale is his godfather as she raises her eyebrows in astonishment. Their happy reunion is abruptly interrupted by the sound of thunderous applause coming from the security monitors.

As they watch the procession of slaves across the stadium floor, Elizabeth tries to withhold tears. Mr. Shale turns to EJ and says, "Son, I need your help. I am too old and disabled to run around like before. However, I promise that if you help me do one last act of sacrifice, tomorrow morning your lives will change for the better. Can you get me onto into that stadium?" They both look at each other and nod.

Elizabeth states, "Mr. Shale I owe you so much. Please allow me to come with you?"

Strategically Positioned...

The wind gusts are pounding much colder air onto Lliam and Emil as they are positioned along the northeast corner of the arena wall. They watch the activities below as more slaves were being paraded onto the arena floor. Emil removes his archery bag from his back.

Sacrifices Are Expensive...

Male slaves, ranging from children to the elderly, march in unison into the arena. Each male is dressed in white. The sight is overwhelming to Eden who is hidden beneath her hooded uniform. She stands alongside the slaves on the arena floor. Once they arrive before the princess, Eden watches them bow low before her cousin.

Eden reflects on a memory of childhood moments when Ilya defended her and showed her love. Those memories are interrupted when Eden sees a male infant being carried to Ilya. Eden recognizes the birthmark on his foot. For the first time, Eden sees Ilya's harmful intentions. In the midst of her anger, Eden calls on help from GOD. "Give me the courage and the strength GOD to rescue that child," she whispers. Ezekiel hears Eden. He has never heard her pray before. She is standing so close to him that he can feel her heartbeat racing.

Almost There...

Elizabeth can see that Mr. Shale is struggling in his efforts to make it to the arena before it is too late. She grabs hold of his forearm and insists that he stop to rest.

He braces himself against her to catch his breath. "We cannot afford to stop," he gasps.

Elizabeth helps him into a sitting position. "Mr. Shale, calm down. Let me go get you water." Mr. Shale shakes his head vigorously.

"There is no time," he states. Elizabeth realizes that his hand is trembling. She hugs him to comfort him. "If you want your son back, then I am your only hope. Please just help me reach the princess." Elizabeth nods.

The Proposal...

Eden watches intently as Ilya addresses the crowd. She recognizes the look of admiration in the women's eyes as they hang onto every word that comes from her cousin's mouth. She can see her former self in every one of them as Ilya speaks to their fears.

"My sisters, because of my grandmother, our queen, we have not only been spared the cruelties of the male species. We have not only survived their abuses. We succeeded in rejecting their systems of hate, violence and rejection and we have created a new world devoid fear. Every day I see smiles, freedom and success throughout our citadel because you all walk with your heads held high. There is no one opposing any of you. There is no one oppressing any of you," Ilya declares.

Ilya continues. "As your new leader, I want to pass this same future onto our sisters and daughters in this life. We must eliminate all threats to the freedom of women." Eden notices that the women are nodding and affirming her statements. "As your leader, my first responsibility is to protect all of your from any threat," Ilya says as she turns and looks at the baby.

A Father's Fury...

While awaiting the command from Lliam, Emil draws his bow. The intensity of his concentration combined with nervousness causes drops of sweat to fall into his eyes. Nonetheless, they maintain focus onto the arena floor.

Lliam can hardly breathe as he watches Ilya approach his son. He swallows and adjusts his vision. "GOD rescue my son," he prays.

Males Are Not To Be Spared...

Ilya draws near to the infant, but stops short. Eden notices that Ilya seems intimidated by the child because she begins to retreat. Eden has never witnessed such an act of fear from her cousin before. Ilya then turns to Vayl and commands that the infant be placed on the sterile altar. No sound could be heard throughout the arena.

Ilya begins to speak. "We are not a brutal society. We have proven time and time again how much we value life. Unfortunately, many of our male species, despite how much we show them kindness, despite how much we attempt to reform them, cannot help but show signs of their violent and destructive nature. This is their true and inherent nature. We have no way left to save such creatures as these." The crowd looks on in silence.

"You are very wrong, princess!" A male voice shouts amidst the slaves. Without hesitation, every guard sets their weapon against Ezekiel who is no longer bowing.

Just In Time...

"Wait!" Lliam orders Emil. Lliam tries to adjust his vision once more as he peers through his small telescope. He then sees Elizabeth entering onto the floor of the arena with Mr. Shale. His eyes widen.

Not a Sound...

Ilya begins to express anger in her tone. "What did you say to me, slave?" Ilya asks Ezekiel as she steps forward.

With boldness he states, "I give my life in exchange for the life of the child that you desire to destroy." Eden begins to find strength in witnessing Ezekiel's actions. She watches her cousin step down from the platform to approach Ezekiel with the support of the guards.

"Who are you to dare to contest me? You are a slave. You are a male designed for destruction. Your life has no worth and neither does this child," Ilya asserts.

Ezekiel is breathing rapidly in apprehension as Ilya moves closer. "What about the life of a princess, is that of any value?" At these words, Ezekiel finds the presence of Princess Ilya intimidating because she stands with her face inches away from his body. Her body is so close that he can smell her perfume. Ezekiel does his best to avoid making direct eye contact because it is forbidden. He maintains his gaze above Ilya's head since his frame is so much taller than hers.

Ilya's breathing is full of anger and control. She demands, "What is this you speak of, slave?"

Courageously, Eden steps toward Ilya and removes the hood. Ilya stands in disbelief at the sight of Eden revealing herself. "How did you escape," Ilya asks. That is when Amblin and Ms. Vivian step forward and remove their hoods also. All face Ilya in silence.

Miracle of Technology...

EJ maintains his focus despite what was occurring on the monitors. He enters several series of codes in an effort to short circuit the electronic shackles on the slaves.

We Are Family...

Ms. Vivian takes a stand next to Eden and faces Ilya. Ilya looks at Amblin and then looks at Vayl before returning her attention to her cousin, Eden. "Well, I see that the family is reunited," Ilya sarcastically retorts.

Eden responds, "Despite your efforts, yes. You are bent on destroying lives. You tried to take my life. Now, you want to destroy an innocent child. I cannot let you do this, Ilya. Whether male or female, this baby has the right to live." Ilya takes deep breaths in anger.

Ilya remarks, "You have always been weak since we were kids. It has been so exhausting having to constantly take care of you, protect you and comfort you. But I had to show grandmother that I could be responsible for you, despite the fact that you proved yourself to be a coward." Eden contains her emotions.

Ilya persists. "We are all aware of your cowardice and your acts of betrayal, Eden. You run from everything that frightens you. You remain silent because you have no idea how persuade or lead. Grandmother would have never selected you to govern. You had nothing to offer then. You have nothing to offer to anyone now."

Eden struggles through embarrassment inflicted upon her in light of Ilya's words. She glances at the look on Ezekiel's face and tries to find the words to respond.

Ezekiel states, "Eden is far from being a coward." His comment is met with anger when Ilya slaps his face for speaking.

The guards prepare themselves. "Bow down slave!" Ilya orders before she slaps him again. Ezekiel continues to stand. Ilya's anger grows. She raises her hand to strike him again, but Eden grabs her wrist. "No more!" Eden commands as she trembles with anger and sweat.

The Task At Hand...

EJ frantically continues to type until a welcomed voice heard coming from the doorway interrupts him. He looks up to see Pastor Eli standing before him. "Dad, you're okay," EJ says as he rises from the chair elated.

Pastor Eli holds up his hand to stop his son from moving closer. "Son, I love you too, but you must continue working. You have a huge task ahead of you," he says.

EJ says, "But dad I have been trying to set these men free. I need help to succeed at this task."

Pastor Eli replies, "That is not the task that I was referring to. I was referring to the task of you saving your sisters."

EJ is overwhelmed. He asks his father, "What sisters?" Suddenly, EJ gets distracted by sounds coming from the crowd on the monitors. "Dad you must come and witness this chaos on this screen," EJ says. EJ points to the monitors to observe the princess, Eden and Ezekiel standing close together in confrontation.

EJ looks back at the doorway to motion his father inside to view the monitors only to look up and see that Pastor Eli is gone. EJ in a panic runs to the doorway and calls out to find his father. The echo of his voice along the empty corridor is the only thing that returns to him.

EJ walks slowly back to the monitors. He wipes tears from his eyes before he freezes one of the frames. He then finds himself staring at both Eden and Ilya on the screen. He recalls his father's voice in his head telling him "Save your sisters".

No More...

Ilya's anger amplifies as she resists Eden's grip. Eden releases her wrist. Eden finds the strength to speak.

"No more, Ilya. No more. No more manipulation. No more exploitation. No more deceit. No more persecution. No more false accusations. No more games. You are done. For years you have blamed everyone else for every miserable ill in this life. And you have blamed me for your own. Now, you are trying to blame an innocent baby for every future ill?" Eden asks.

The anger on Ilya's face is evident as Eden continues speaking. "To add insult to injury, you are trying to persuade all of these women to believe that destroying infants simply because they are males is what is best for them. You cannot be serious. This makes no sense. This was not what our mothers or our grandmother set out to accomplish. You know that."

Eden steps closer to Ilya with her hands raised up in submission in an attempt to prove that she is no threat. Eden confirms, "Ilya, this is me, your cousin, your blood. I love you. I know more than anyone how much you have longed to become queen. I want that for you. But, I cannot allow you to harm innocent people. It is not necessary, Ilya," Eden says.

Ilya can no longer contain her rage. She feels embarrassed before the crowd at what Eden stated. "I hate you! I hate both of you!" Ilya yells. That is when Ilya points. Eden is initially hurt by Ilya's verbal attack. However, she finds herself confused once she realizes that Ilya is not pointing at her or Ezekiel. Ilya is pointing at Mr. Shale.

Saying Goodbye...

EJ walks slowly around the engineering room. He feels cold. Finding himself too afraid to say the words aloud, he returns to his stance in front of the security monitors. A worn sheet of linen paper sits with the number "0-31742" and the words "but a mist on this side" written.

EJ holds the fragile piece of paper in his hand, thus lifting it to his nose to inhale. He immediately recognizes the scent and begins to type the sequence of numbers into the computer frame. It is the code to release the slaves from the shackles. The tears fall from EJ's eyes because he notices that the sequence of numbers is his father's birthdate. That is when he realizes that his father has died. "I will see you on the other side too," he whispers.

Chains Are Broken...

The sky overhead grows windy and dark with storm clouds. A surge in power overtakes the arena. Suddenly, the sound of shackles unlocking can be heard. As the male slaves began to recognize they are unbound, one by one they start to stand. Immediately, the guards surround them and prepare for combat.

Only One Truth...

Mr. Shale and Elizabeth draw closer to Eden's side in order to face Ilya. Mr. Shale tries to catch his breath before he speaks. With humility and respect, he addresses Ilya. "Your mother, your grandmother and your father all agreed that you would make a regal princess someday," Mr. Shale says.

Ilya demands, "Why do you dare mention my father?"

Mr. Shale humbly replies, "Because, he has been the source of your anger for your entire life, princess." Ilya shakes her head in disagreement.

Mr. Shale states that it is indeed true. "I have known you and your family your entire life, princess. Your father has been my best friend since he and I were kids. He kept nothing hidden from me. Granted, I know the source of your bitterness, because I know you." Ilya stands virtually paralyzed before Mr. Shale. She can offer no reaction to his statements.

"It was no secret that your mother and father were very much in love. Their relationship was quite endearing. Your father clearly adored your mother," Mr. Shale confirms. "Neither Eden nor her mother, Princess Dianne, are to blame for any crime you feel was committed against your mother." Eden finds herself confused at his statement.

"Before either you or Eden existed, the relationship between Princess Dianne, Princess Dana and your father, Pastor Eli, became a complicated triangle. Shortly before the war, your father was to become our next king. But, his mother, Lady Nancy, made it very clear that he would not be allowed to take your mother, Princess Dana, as his wife. She questioned your mother's purity." Ilya breathes rapidly in anger and slight embarrassment.

Mr. Shale further explains. "Your father was devastated by his mother's accusations. He had never been with your mother. He also knew that your mother had never been with another man. Yet, somehow, Lady Nancy had convinced him to question Princess Dana's purity all because she was so much more animated and spirited in nature in comparison to her more modest sister, Dianne."

Mr. Shale moves closer to Ilya. "Your father was so distraught. Instead of defending your mother, he distanced himself. She became ill at the loss of his love. Your grandmother tried to protect Princess Dana's heart and reputation. She even tried to reason with Lady Nancy, but there was no change." At the name of Pastor Eli being identified as her father, Ilya, Ezekiel and Eden were beyond the loss for words.

Taking It In...

EJ sits before the monitors and tries to absorb the details that Mr. Shale is disclosing about his father to Princess Ilya. He is beyond overwhelmed as well. Every word leaves him feeling surprised.

Resting his face in his hands, EJ whispers to himself, "They are my sisters." That's when he realizes that he has lost his father whom he adores and gained two sisters who are enemies. Perplexed, he begins to weep.

Absorbing Truth...

Ilya holds her bottom lip between her teeth as Mr. Shale continues to reveal more truth. "Your mother became so depressed that your grandmother sent her away. During her absence, Pastor Eli and Eden's mother began to develop a bond in response to your mother's absence."

Ilya wiped her tears. "Your paternal grandmother, Lady Nancy, began to grow fond of Eden's mother. It did not take long for a proposal of marriage to occur. Many people assumed that your father only sought to marry Eden's mother because he was suffering a broken heart.

Regardless, while your mother was away, Pastor Eli did marry Eden's mother," Mr. Shale verified.

Ilya shakes her head in hurt and insists, "He did not marry my mother! He is not my father! He is her father!" Ilya yells while pointing at Eden. Mr. Shale counters. "You are correct. He did not marry your mother, but he is your father." Eden's eyes widen.

"Your mother returned immediately when she heard he married her sister. The moment your father saw her again, his love for her also returned stronger than before. It was undeniable. Thus, they had a brief affair which resulted in you," he verified.

"Before you were even born, your mother was consumed with guilt at what she had done to her sister. She felt she had created a chaotic situation for you, her sister, your grandmother and her true love. She took her life which resulted in your father's struggle with his eternal guilt. He knew he had failed your mother when she trusted him. Only instead of such a drastic act as suicide, your father turned his life over to seeking GOD," Mr. Shale said.

"Your father loved your mother deeply. He never rejected her. He never rejected you. He sent me here to tell you that he loved you. He has always loved both of you. He knew he failed you when he abandoned your mother. Your mother died because your father broke her heart. Moreover, your father told me before he died that his cowardice was an example of how men have been hurting women for centuries."

Then, Mr. Shale turns to speak to the males. He says, "Pastor Eli wanted me to also apologize for failing all of you as well. He never became the leader that you all deserved."

He continues, "None of you, male or female, should be standing on this arena floor in chains. You should all be free to grow, to laugh, to learn, to pray, to hope and to love. We men must take responsibility for causing the pain that has driven you women to establish this extreme society."

Mr. Shale next addresses the women. "Every time we crushed your spirits, confused your minds and broke your confidence, we hardened your hearts."

Then Mr. Shale returned his attention to Ilya. "My best friend failed you and your sister. The evidence of that pain was more than clear. It became infectious. Please allow me to sincerely state how truly, truly sorry we men are." He extends his hand and pleads with Ilya. "I know that you may never forgive your father, but please do not take your anger out on one more person, especially on the one person who loves you most, your sister."

The Royal Reaction...

Every person stood in complete silence throughout the arena. Only the gusts of the winds could be heard. Ilya moves closer towards Mr. Shale. He can sense her anger. Ilya erupts. "You were my father's best friend. Then, after the war, you became Eden's personal servant. Now, you claim that you are here because you care about me?" Mr. Shale offers no response.

Ilya maintains that it is no secret where Mr. Shale's loyalties lie. "You did not come here for me. You are here for the sake of your precious Eden." Then Ilya stares at Eden. She states, "You were right. I have hated my father my entire life. But I have hated my cousin even more."

Ilya instructs Vayl to bring her the baby. Vayl complies by collecting the baby and returning beside Ilya. Eden tries to approach Ilya, but Mr. Shale holds her back gently. Eden cautiously asks, "What are you doing, Ilya? He is just a baby."

In arrogance, Ilya responds. "You care more about this infant male slave than you care about me. Don't you? That does not seem like love or loyalty to me." Eden is at a loss as to how to answer. Ilya retorts, "And this would be why we have a serious problem. This is how you betray all of us once again. This is what determines you to be an enemy of our state. And this is why this child must die."

In Slow Motion...

Instantly, Elizabeth charges Vayl in an attempt to save her baby. Ms. Vivian tries to secure Elizabeth, but is unable. Elizabeth seizes her baby away from Vayl. Ilya orders an attack. Within seconds, the slaves begin to scatter and escape. The guards immediately trail them.

Mr. Shale attempts to shield Amblin and Eden. Yet, Amblin yells in an effort to warn Elizabeth that Ilya is drawing near. Within seconds, a series of arrows begin to rain down around them. Ezekiel looks up and sees that the arrows are being shot from above by Emil. Panic and fear ensues throughout the crowd.

The arrows strategically surround Amblin, Eden, Mr. Shale, Elizabeth and Ilya. To protect themselves, they all bow low and cover their heads. Eden gets distracted when she hears a familiar voice.

As chaos overtakes the crowd, Eden rises. She sees the angel again and feels strangely empowered. The next few moments occur virtually in slow motion. Eden who is filled with unexplainable might rushes toward the infant.

Final Price of Freedom...

Elizabeth tries to hold on tightly to her baby while she fends off guards. Ezekiel battles the guards in an effort to help Elizabeth. Eden pushes her way towards the baby. In that moment, she hears Amblin yell. Eden is horrified at the sight of seeing her cousin retrieving one of the arrows. She knows that Ilya desperately wants to destroy the baby.

Eden is determined to reach the infant. With every bit of her strength, she forces her way through the multitude of guards towards the baby. Even though the chaos of the crowd is deafening, she can still hear the baby. As Ezekiel shields Elizabeth and her baby from the violence, Eden wraps herself around Ezekiel. She never feels the arrow invading her.

Time Stands Still...

Eden's eyes widen. She is able to see the baby. As the pain begins to radiate through her spine, she can see the birthmark on the foot of the baby begin to glow.

Ezekiel can feel the warmth of a liquid on his back. He turns and catches Eden, breaking her fall. His mind is unable to comprehend what has happened to her. He takes a moment to glance up only to find Ilya standing before him shaking while holding a bloodied arrow. Ezekiel falls to the ground holding Eden. He hears Amblin screaming for a doctor. In the moment, Ezekiel refuses to cry.

Ezekiel cradles Eden so tight against his chest that she can hear his heartbeat. "You will be fine. Help is coming. You just need to hold on," he assures her. Eden then tries to laugh. She says, "For once in your life, you can please tell the truth. You are not very good at lying." They both smile at each other in an effort to mentally escape this moment of anguish. Eden requests, "If you refuse to tell the truth to me, then promise me that you will teach it to all of these people?"

Ezekiel stares into Eden's eyes. She begins to cough. Blood begins to saturate his legs. Eden grasps Ezekiel's hand. The tears in his eyes visibly convey how pronounced her injuries are and how great his pain is. Thus, she gathers all the strength she has in an effort to speak assuredly.

"You know the irony is that I have only known you less than a few days. Yet, you are the only one I could ask this of. Tomorrow when you wake and this nightmare has ended, would you consider unifying the women and the men? They could use some new leadership and besides I think I am more than ready to resign from my royal duties." Eden knows that Ezekiel is hesitant to laugh. She continues, "Let me warn you that this job as a royal leader is bit hazardous. My cousin may try to kill you." Ezekiel smiles as his tears fall onto her forehead.

Ezekiel responds, "I have never heard you say the word 'men' before as if you now see us as humans." Then he asks, "Why did you do that? Why did you protect me? I am a slave here."

Eden gently shakes her head and reminded him, "You are not my slave. You are my friend. Remember when we were at the cabin, you said that men and women can be just friends."

A light begins to blind her vision. Eden realizes that the glare is radiating from a little boy standing over her. She closes her eyes.

The little boy is dressed in white. "Haven't we met before?" Eden asks. The little boy smiles and extends his hand to her. Eden breathes her last and dies.

Exiting The Arena...

Ezekiel rises while holding Eden's body. Ilya begins ranting. "What are you doing? Where do you think you are going with my cousin?" she screams before she realizes she misspoke. Ezekiel continues to move forward with Eden in silence. Ilya pauses briefly before she attempts to yell while correcting her previous statement, "I command that you put my sister down!" The noise and confusion of the crowd begins to still. Ilya continues to yell in frustration and agitation. Ezekiel walks past Ilya, but she refuses to be dismissed.

Ilya quickly positions herself in front of him in order to block him. Her actions are so erratic and unstable that it draws the attention of the crowd.

Ilya demands, "Stop I say!" She suddenly confronts Ezekiel by striking his face. The crowd is silenced. The imprint of her blow begins to cause Ezekiel's face to redden. Tears fall from his eyes. "You are to obey me, slave!" Ilya screams. "Put her down! I said put her down!" Yet, Ezekiel stands before Ilya unmoved. Ilya then tries to intimidate Ezekiel. "Are you prepared to die for her?" Ilya asks.

Ezekiel finally breaks his silence, "You have already killed her. Your sister is dead, princess. You can kill me if you so desire, but I am taking her with me."

Ilya panics at his words. "She is not dead! She is just unconscious. She needs a doctor. Let me see her. Let me see my sister!" she demands. Ezekiel refuses. Many of the women have never witnessed a male showing such concern for one of them. They start to cry.

Ilya tries to face the crowd and explain. "It was an accident. She is fine." Then, she begs Ezekiel to allow her to touch Eden. He allows Ilya to draw close enough to touch her face. Ilya breaks at the sudden reality of losing her grandmother, the only man she has loved and her cousin within this day. She falls to her knees weeping. Amblin and Ms. Vivian are speechless.

Ezekiel, still holding Eden's lifeless body, faces the crowd. Vayl approaches him. Without saying a word, she bows before Ezekiel and allows him to pass. One by one, each guard begins to respectfully bow. The crowd then parts and kneels. They allow Ezekiel to carry Eden's body out of the arena.

Ezekiel ignores the faces in the crowd as he walks by. He can feel the grains of gravel under his feet with each step. His anguish is evident. As Ezekiel walks he recalls memories of her. He exits the arena. His walk is long.

A "Newer" World...

The spring rains seemed to add so much life to the garden. "Be careful, Shale! Wait for mommy," Elizabeth instructs. At age 7, Shale moved quickly through the garden. It was difficult for Elizabeth to keep up in her in her third trimester. Elizabeth called for her son again when he disappeared. There was no response. Before she could panic, she hears his laughter.

As the trees part, she sees Shale embracing his father. Elizabeth smiles at the sight of seeing Lliam and Emil completing the construction of the monument. Elizabeth is greeted with an endearing hello. "What do you think?" Amblin asks. "Did our men do a great job, or what?"

Elizabeth stares at the names on the monument amidst the garden. "I wish Eden were here to see this," Amblin says as she kisses Emil. Then Amblin reminds everyone that they all have a standing appointment with a certain bride and groom. "You know that Ilya will kill us if we are late to her wedding." Emil replies, "Ezekiel will not care if we are late."

Lliam teases, "Would you prefer to attend his wedding or his funeral?"

Emil confirms, "Enough said, let's not risk starting yet another war." They all laugh. EJ says, "It is time to see how the rest of this day unfolds and bid farewell to our Garden of Eden."

Not Necessarily The End...

Made in the USA
Lexington, KY
31 January 2017